The Christmas Wish

The Christmas Wish

A Canadays of Montana Romance

Barbara Ankrum

The Christmas Wish

Tule Publishing First Printing, October 2016

The Tule Publishing Group, LLC

Dedication

To my parents, who always loved Christmas.

"And above all, watch with glittering eyes the whole world around you because the greatest secrets are always hidden in the most unlikely places. Those who don't believe in magic will never find it."

~Roald Dahl~

Chapter One

"TELL HIM HOW you feel. What are you waiting for?" Eve Canaday's stepsister, Olivia, tucked a string of twinkly, white lights around the trunk of one of the bare white trees inside the Graff Hotel ballroom then handed the strand up to Eve, who was standing on a ladder above her. "I mean, what's the worst that can happen?"

Eve sighed, wrapping the strand of lights around the thin, white branches. "The worst is he laughs and pats me on the head like I'm hilarious. Until he realizes I mean it and he runs for the nearest exit."

Olivia chuckled, her blonde hair glimmering in the winking lights. "Pats you on the head? First of all, he's only what? Six years older than you? So, that's nothing. And second, lots of men are commitment-phobes until they meet the right woman."

"That's just it. He doesn't think of me as a woman. To him, I'm just a friend. A buddy." Eve clapped a hand on her chest. "I am *not* a buddy, Livvy. I have *breasts*. Not that he's noticed."

She laughed. "Um… I've seen him looking at you. I think he definitely has noticed."

"Really?" Eve sighed. "Then he's just not interested."

"Maybe you're just afraid to find out if he really is or if he isn't."

"What? Me? I am *not*." Because if she'd neglected to stand on her head to get him to take her seriously, well, there was only so far she was willing to go in this standoff. Shouldn't he meet her at least halfway?

"I'm just sayin'…" Olivia said as she untangled a knot of lights.

Eve shook her head. "No. That's the wrong approach with him. He's complicated. And skittish."

"Maybe you're both just afraid to mess up a good friendship. But clearly, it's fish or cut bait time for you, Evie," her sister said. "If you're unhappy with how it's going, change it."

Eve sighed and sat back on the ladder, wondering if Olivia was right. She scanned the activity in the ballroom she'd been hired to stage for the Marietta Christmas Ball. The room was beginning to look like the Christmas fantasy she'd envisioned—a forest, all magically lit for Christmas. Staged with bare, white trees awaiting twinkling white lights and traditional, towering green spruce, already beribboned and hung with sparkling ornaments and snow. Boxes stacked along the walls held the remainder of the decorations and a handful of Eve's team of stagers was busy unpacking them.

There were ladders and bubble wrap scattered across the floor and, despite the Christmas music being piped into the ballroom, almost everyone wore earbuds and was in their own musical world as they worked. The ball was three short days away.

And she would be going alone.

Pathetic.

"You make that sound so easy. Just because your Jake thinks the sun rises and sets on you." Eve handed back the end of the strand to connect the plug to the next.

Jake Lassen, Olivia's gorgeous helicopter pilot fiancé, had come looking for Olivia after ten years in the military and would stop at nothing to make her his. Her other sister, Kate, had settled with bull-rider Finn Scott and his twins, a match no one saw coming, but one that was solid as a rock now.

"You and Kate cannot be my standard bearers for relationships. Because you're both anomalies and, frankly, that's just depressing and a lot to live up to."

"Nobody expects you to live up to anything," Olivia said, handing up another string of lights. "And let's face it, I'm no exception to any rule. You know how my first marriage ended."

Olivia's first husband had been her mentor/trainer on the way to the Olympic equestrian team, but her dreams had been cut short by a bad accident. Her marriage hadn't survived the accident either, but one door opened when another one closed, as the saying went. And Jake had walked right in.

"You know," Olivia went on, "Jake's and my relationship was far from a cakewalk. But one thing I did learn—I was usually flat out wrong when I tried to guess what he was thinking. So now, I ask. So, don't be a goose. Look around you, Eve." She gestured at the ballroom. "*This* is amazing. You are amazing and any guy would be lucky to have you. If he can't see that, well..."

Eve's phone pinged with a text and she looked down at it. "Speak of the devil. I guess he's finally out of his surgery. I promised him a ride to the airport today. He's leaving for Roatan. Dive tour."

"Tell him I think his timing sucks." Olivia held the ladder for Eve as she climbed down.

With a sigh, she answered, "I agree. Thanks for coming over to help."

"Sure." Olivia hugged her. "I can't wait to see the finished product. It's going to be incredible when you're done. As always. And I can't wait to see what you do for our wedding."

Eve hugged her. "Thanks. Me, too. And thanks for the advice. I'll think about what you said. Really, I will."

"And then you'll do the exact opposite."

Eve shrugged with a grin. "Possibly."

She laughed. "See you later at Lane's End? Mom's cooking lasagna tonight."

"I should be back in time. It would take more than Ben Tyler to make me miss her lasagna. See you then."

BEN TYLER COULDN'T help but smile at Eve from the passenger seat of her car. She'd been chatting away for a few minutes about nothing in particular and for some weird reason, he got the sense she was nervous today. Nervous around him. She was so darned cute when she got chatty like this. Because she had a way of making him laugh over nothing and he couldn't remember another woman ever doing that before.

You should just tell her the truth.

"So I called them back"—Eve went on—"this company I ordered from, and told them that no matter how many fake eggs they sent me to fill those horrid baskets they'd 'inadvertently' substituted, they would still look like a herd of geese had accidentally chosen my party for a nesting spot. Seriously."

He chuckled. "Gaggle."

"Huh?"

"A *gaggle* of geese."

"Oh. Right. I should have told them that. But they did refund me."

"Atta girl." Ben stretched his leg as far as he could under the dash, just then noticing the dark clouds lurking on the western horizon. In the next instant, he heard Eve's sudden intake of breath, saw the swoop of something flashing in front of the car and then—

"Hang on!" Eve cried.

Ben braced himself as the wheels of Eve's SUV veered suddenly across the icy mountain pass highway toward a snowy ditch on the side of the road. The antlered streak of brown that had vaulted in front of the car, disappeared like a shadow… along with any chance of him making his flight.

Time slowed instantly to a crawl. The camera of his vision took in every small instant of the skid like an old fashioned flip book.

Tick. He swung a look at Eve, fighting the icy road for control. The look on her face made him—*tick*—reach a protective hand out to her and realize—*tick*—he didn't give a flying damn about his flight!

Bam!

The snowbank exploded against the front end of her car accompanied by the crunch of metal and a sucker punch to the face from the airbag.

And everything went quiet, except for the rhythmic creak of the engine in the muffled depths of the snowbank.

Stunned, he muttered a curse and coughed as the airbag deflated. He waved away the powdery white stuff floating in the air. Still seeing stars, he winced, running his tongue along a fresh cut in his lip. His chest lurched as he flicked a look at Eve, who, like him, was pitched forward against her shoulder harness, still shaking off the impact.

He touched her shoulder and she flinched in surprise. "Eve, you hurt?"

She looked dazed, trying to catch her breath as she rubbed a fist against her chest. A reddish scrape had already begun swelling near her right eye.

She touched her cheek gingerly. "No. I don't think so. Nothing broken but my pride. And apparently, my car." Her eyes turned suspiciously glassy and she blinked away tears.

Already the abrasion on her cheek had started to bruise. Still stuck in his seatbelt, he had the weirdest impulse to pull her against him and make everything all right. His fault, for agreeing to let her to drive him to the airport on these roads today. Why hadn't he just called a cab?

"That was no deer. I could have sworn it was a—" Her eyes widened. "Oh, Ben… you're bleeding!"

Swiping at his chin, his fingers encountered moisture and came back bloody. "That's the last time I feel anything less than pure compassion for anyone in my ER who's been coldcocked by one of these air bags."

She turned a mortified look his way. "We'll never make it to the airport now. Oh, Ben—your trip…"

He reached over and shut off the engine. "That thing could be sitting in our laps right now if you hadn't swerved to avoid hitting it."

"That *thing* being a—?"

"Reindeer." Ben pointed to a stand of Ponderosa pines a few dozen feet off the side of the road in the gloaming light of the oncoming storm. The unscathed culprit stood under the trees, wearing a glittery green and red halter, decorated with jingle bells, like an escapee from Santa's Christmas barn. Calmly, it chewed on the bare branches of some underlying shrubs and occasionally deigned to glance in their direction, making his harness jingle.

"Ohh-hh," Eve muttered, narrowing a look at the animal. "Will you just look at him, standing there, all cheery and Christmassy?" Her window made a grinding sound as she rolled it down. "Hey! Thank you!" she shouted over the virgin drifts of snow on the side of the road. "No really, go on and eat. Don't mind us. We had nothing better to do today than sit in a snowbank!"

He grinned, then winced at his split lip. "*Ow.* Don't make me laugh."

She flicked an apologetic grin back at him. "I'm so sorry, Ben. I've screwed everything up for you. Do you think they'll hold the boat for you in Roatan if you're late?"

The boat, presumably taking him on a "dive tour," sounded like a lot more fun than what he'd really been about to do in Central America. Digging himself deeper in the lie he'd already told Eve about this trip was something he'd hoped to avoid, but he was already in this far. And now seemed like the absolute wrong time to confess.

So, he said, "My connections were pretty tight and unchangeable. Flights into the country are so limited, once I miss my flights, it'll be impossible to catch up with them.

They're scheduled to leave tomorrow morning for ten days. They won't wait for me." That much was true.

He sighed, already dreading the phone call he'd have to make to Dr. Camran in Honduras when they got back to town. *If* he could even reach him.

She looked stricken. "We're only twenty-five minutes or so from Marietta. I'll call one of my sisters. Maybe there's time for one of them to come and—"

But the bars on his cell phone were nonexistent. "No service. We're in a dead zone here in the mountain pass. I drive this way all the time to the hospital up in Bozeman. It's dead or spotty at best here for two miles or more. And weather is moving in fast."

Indeed, the gunmetal sky had grown darker.

"Well," she said, staring at the miscreant reindeer, "if Santa's anywhere nearby, we could use a Christmas miracle because this car is not getting anyone anywhere. Not even back to Marietta." She sighed. "I mean, please, who gets run off the road by Rudolph?"

Me. Ben zipped up his heavy parka over the scuba geek tee Jake had given him that read, "*The deeper you go, the better it feels.*" Appropriate on some future trip to paradise, but he'd worn it for the sake of the lie he'd told everyone. Not even Jake knew what he was up to.

This whole fiasco was on him, really. If he hadn't cut things so close. A last minute emergency surgery had pared his schedule down to the bone and now the whole trip was blown because of a freaking reindeer.

Perfect.

Eve wrestled to get her door open, past the snow wedged underneath. She managed a six-inch crack. "Ugh. I am such an idiot, wrecking my car the one time I—" She stopped short and a blush crept up her cheeks, as if she'd admitted more than she'd meant to.

"It's my fault, not yours," he said. "I should've given myself more time. I have travel insurance. I'll rebook it for another time."

"I know, but," she said, with a wistful sigh, "warm beaches… tropical drinks… coral reefs versus"—she gestured out the freezing window—"five degrees below zero and snow in the forecast." She sighed. "On the bright side, at least there's Christmas in Marietta."

He glanced off at the drifting snow. *Exactly.* "Yeah." Even as he watched, the four-legged fulcrum of all this trouble trotted off, unconcerned, into the forest. In his best Michael Corleone voice, he muttered, "*Just when I thought I was out, they pull me back in!*"

She tilted an amused look at him. "I don't think Christmas in Marietta was what Mario Puzzo had in mind when he wrote that line."

"What? You mean the Whoville of Montana? The North Pole of the lower forty-eight?"

"I wouldn't go that far."

"Oh, I would. There's no escaping holiday cheer in that

place. No dodging city blocks of happy Christmas lights, or red and green displays in every shop window, or apparently, even reindeer running wild."

"Hmm. I definitely heard a bah-humbug in there," she said, fingering her injured cheek.

"I'd make an effort to deny it," he said, shoving his own door partway open against the snowbank, "but this might not be the best time."

Acknowledging his point with a nod, she shivered as frigid air poured through her open window and she tugged her gloves out of her coat pockets. "So, to clarify, the holiday-ish timing of your trip wasn't—"

"Coincidental?" he finished. "Nope."

She tipped her head. "Huh."

He gave up on his door and slammed it shut again. The snowbank they'd buried the front end in collapsed on the hood and a chunk of snow slid down the windshield with a *splat*.

Outside, big, fat flakes began to settle against the glass, slowly at first, then furiously. It began pouring in her open window.

"Oh, look. It's snowing," she said, catching flakes in her bare hand. "I suppose they'll find us in the spring when the snow melts. Maybe Rudolph will guide them with his nose-so-bright to our tragically buried car."

"Or"—Ben forced the mechanism on his seat belt and caught himself with a hand on the dashboard—"we could climb out your open window and flag down someone for help."

"Yeah," she agreed, "that would be a happier ending."

But it took almost another half-hour before another vehicle braved the pass in the storm. It was a semi, heading toward Marietta and the driver radioed a tow truck for them and let them wait in his heated truck cabin. By then, both were chilled to the bone.

When they finally made it back to town, the sun was on its way down. The tow truck driver—a sweet local named Nolan Weeks—asked them where they wanted to be dropped before he took her car to the repair shop. Ben told him to go to the hospital.

"I left my car parked there," he said to Eve. "I'll give you a ride home."

"Why don't you come out to Lane's End? Stay for dinner. Shake this off. I hear they're doing a lasagna thing tonight. They were expecting me anyway and they'd love to have you."

He and Eve had become good friends a year ago, after meeting at her father's birthday party, an event his old friend Jake Lassen had dragged him to and his friendship with Eve had bloomed after that night.

He wasn't exactly sure why it had never gone farther. Why they'd never slept together. It wasn't as if he hadn't thought about it. He definitely had. Like the rest of the Canaday sisters, Eve was so pretty, sometimes, he found himself just staring at her when she wasn't looking. But he supposed it was because she wasn't the sort of girl one messed with without serious intentions. She was the kind of girl one married.

That was… someone would marry her, but it wouldn't be him. He was already in a committed relationship with medicine. That was as much of a promise as he could manage.

Even so, with the reality of how close they'd come to disaster today finally settling over him, he felt grateful he hadn't cost Eve more than a banged up car and a few bruises. The least he could do was be sociable with her family. Apologize in person.

"Okay," he said. "That sounds good. I'll just check in before I go. Tell the powers that be that I'm not taking a vacation after all."

"You know," she said, touching his arm, "you deserve a vacation. You work too hard. People actually pay money to come to Marietta at Christmastime. To feel part of the traditions here. It's a destination."

He smiled at her. "I grew up here, remember? I know the drill. At Christmastime, I'd rather be somewhere else."

EVE WAS STILL puzzling over his words as she sat in the tinseled red and green nurses' station, visiting with Kelly Reynolds, an old friend of hers from high school. Still single, like Eve, and now a nurse, Kelly suffered from the same unwavering dedication to her job that Ben did and she'd shooed Ben away, insisting on cleaning up the abrasion on Eve's cheek herself. Now, while Eve waited for Ben to finish checking in with the chief of staff, she wondered what was taking him so long?

"Owee! That stings!" she complained as Kelly dabbed her cheek with antiseptic.

"Don't be a baby." Kelly teased. "You're very lucky it wasn't worse. I've seen elk go through windshields before."

"I know. We were lucky. But it wasn't an elk. It was a reindeer."

"We don't have reindeer down here, do we?"

"Wearing sparkly, jingle-bell halters? Apparently so. Know if any have escaped Santa's sleigh at the Christmas tree lot?"

Kelly tucked a loose auburn strand of hair back into her pony tail. "What do I know? I never get out of this place. I'm like a willing hostage to my job. I do remember that tree lot though with the reindeer. I used to love it as a kid. I was pretty sure if I sat on that particular Santa's lap, I'd get what I wanted for Christmas. Those reindeer were just the burden of proof I needed to believe. But the one you saw must have travelled far afield to get up to the pass where you were."

"I know, right? We were really in the middle of nowhere."

"You and Dr. Tyler. What's up with that?" Kelly asked

with a grin. "You two seeing each other?"

"No." She sighed. "We're just friends. I was just giving him a ride to the airport."

"Uh-huh. But a ride to the airport"—Kelly explained, dabbing more antibiotic cream on Eve's cheek—"is more than a ride to the airport. It's dating code."

"It is?" Eve asked, as if she didn't know.

"It's like… I'll take you to the airport, but that means I'll be here when you get back. It's a clear message."

Said code had clearly skipped directly over Ben's head. "Wonder what the message is when I nearly kill him on the way?"

Kelly smiled. "But you didn't."

"But I almost did."

"That would have certainly broken a bunch of hearts around here. But I should warn you, he's got a reputation."

"Oh?" she asked innocently, though she'd definitely heard about the infamous Dr. Tyler from scuttlebutt around town.

Which was probably why he never gave her an actual second look—that way. He was too busy being chased by nurses and female doctors with agendas.

"Yeah," Kelly went on. "Commitment-phobe. But I suppose if you're built like him, with skills like his, why choose?"

Eve answered with a weak laugh. *Indeed.* "So… you're not saying he's a man-whore?"

The other woman laughed. "We definitely have a few of those here, but Dr. Tyler doesn't fall into that category. No, he's more of an enigma, wrapped in a mystery, all bundled in a sexy, healthy package. I can count on one hand the women who've fallen in his wake. But," she said, leaning closer, "none of them is really complaining, if you know what I mean."

Okay then! "Speaking of which, any clue what's keeping him? We're supposed to be meeting my parents for dinner at their place."

Kelly arched a knowing eyebrow about the "*dinner with parents*" thing just as the answer to Eve's question came hurrying down the hallway on a squeak of white soles. A surgical nurse in blue scrubs who Eve didn't recognize came toward them, holding a young girl in her arms.

Eve straightened. If she wasn't mistaken that was Patsy Sherman's four-year-old daughter, Lily. But Malcom, the little girl's widowed dad, was nowhere in sight.

Oh, no. Two very bad things couldn't happen on the same day, surely. But a moment later, the nurse confirmed her worst fears. She only heard snatches of the conversation as the nurse set the girl down on the waiting room couch across the way and spoke to Kelly.

"Hanging the Christmas lights… bad fall… on-call doctor is in another surgery… take care of her until we can figure this out. Apparently the mom isn't in the picture."

That last seemed to Eve a cruel way to point out that

Malcom and Lily had lost Patsy halfway through last January to breast cancer, leaving them alone. Eve's heart sank at the thought that Lily could have actually lost her father, too. The little girl looked red-eyed, like she'd been crying, but now she just sat silently, with her knees up under her chin and her arms wrapped around her skinny little legs.

So, that was where Ben was. One of three go-to orthopedic guys at Marietta Regional Hospital and on staff at several others nearby, Ben was known for innovative surgery most other doctors wouldn't even attempt. If anyone could fix Malcom's broken bones, he could. Maybe there was a reason she'd driven that car into a snowbank this afternoon.

The surgical nurse, whose name badge read Katrina, hurried to her next. "You're Eve Canaday?"

"That's right."

"Dr. Tyler asked me to tell you that he's going into surgery and won't be able to make it to your parents' house and that he's terribly sorry. He had me call a cab for you."

Did he now? "If you wouldn't mind, please cancel the cab. I'll sit with Lily until her dad's out of surgery. How bad is it?"

Katrina flicked a look at Kelly who nodded. "He was mostly alert and talking. That's always good sign with a head injury. But he'll take some healing after the surgery on his broken bones."

"What about Lily? Any relatives nearby? Can we call someone?"

"There's no one else, according to Mr. Sherman. Actually, he asked Dr. Tyler personally to look after her."

Ben? Oh, God. She'd almost forgotten that he and Malcolm were old friends. "What did Dr. Tyler say?"

The nurse sighed. "Nothing definite, but I can't imagine how he would have time for such a thing. He barely eats."

"Technically"—Eve pointed out—"he is on vacation. He isn't even supposed to be here right now."

"Lucky for Mr. Sherman, he is," Kelly said.

"He'd be great with her," Eve said, looking at the little girl curling into a ball on the couch. Katrina and Kelly exchanged looks. She knew what they were thinking. He was a surgeon, not a babysitter. "*What*? He would," Eve said. "You just don't know him like I do."

Kelly nodded sagely. "Mm-hmm."

"I don't mean that way. I just mean—oh, never mind. Katrina, could you please let us know when Malcolm is out of surgery?"

"Sure, dear. And I'll tell him you're staying," Katrina said, then hustled back in the direction of the OR.

Eve looked over at Lily who was shivering. She turned to Kelly. "Can I get a blanket? Something soft?"

Kelly disappeared and returned a moment later from the linen closet with a not-terribly-soft-but-would-do-in-a-pinch hospital blanket.

Eve sat down beside the little girl who was fingering a long, white feather, wrapped on the end with a leather tie.

"Hi, Lily. Do you remember me? I'm Eve. We've met before. I'm a friend of your mommy and daddy."

Lily said nothing. She simply twirled the feather between her fingers.

"Your mommy and I went to school together when we were little girls like you. Did you know that?" Lily shook her head. "What do you say we take your jacket off? Personally, there's nothing I like better than cuddling up in a warm blanket when I'm feeling sad. How about you?"

Slowly, so as not to spook her, Eve helped her out of her heavy winter coat, then unfolded the blanket and draped it over Lily's small form. The girl clutched it tightly under her chin.

"And when you get nice and toasty, I happen to know where they sell the best ice cream in Marietta. It's right down the hall in the cafeteria." She crossed her heart and smiled. Lily still refused to look at her. "No? That's okay. Maybe later. Mind if I share your blanket?"

IT WAS NEARLY midnight before Ben found her in the waiting room, beside Lily, who had fallen sound asleep across Eve's lap. Eve was asleep, too, head tilted against the sofa back. His breath caught as he stood in the doorway at the sight of her dark hair cascading down the porcelain of her cheek. That little line of freckles that ran across her nose made him swallow hard and take a deep breath.

Her hand was resting on the child's shoulder, a picture of a woman meant to be a mother someday. He was still in scrubs and he ran a hand tiredly down his face, rubbing his eyes. It had been an incredibly long day and it wasn't over yet. But the conundrum of the child still balanced on the scale in his mind. He'd walked in here intending to ask Eve to take Lily home. To take responsibility for her. After all, Eve had been Patsy's friend, too. And though he was Mal's friend from way back, surely, given the choice between himself and Eve, Mal would choose Eve. Surely.

But he'd asked *him*. And seeing her now with the child in her lap—a task she'd taken on without being asked—it seemed unfair to ask her to do more.

The object of his thoughts roused and opened her eyes. With a sharp intake of breath, she nearly sat up, before remembering the child in her lap. Cautiously, she untangled herself from the girl and walked over to him.

"How's Malcom?"

"He'll heal. He's sporting some extra metal in his femur and his wrist. Luckily for him, he didn't fracture his pelvis. Just a bad contusion. He'll be in here for a while with that head trauma though."

"Thank God he'll be okay."

"She fell asleep," he said, gesturing at Lily.

"She's exhausted."

"So are you."

"I wasn't the one standing up doing surgery all night after a car accident. I was tucked under my comfy blankie with my little friend. *You* are exhausted."

But her hair was tangled and her eye makeup was smudged.

He kind of liked her rumpled look. "I'll take you home."

"What about Lily?"

"I'll take her to my place."

"So, you're going to do it? Take care of her, I mean?"

He nodded. "I will until I can make other arrangements. It shouldn't take more than a day or so."

"What other arrangements?"

He hadn't thought that far ahead, yet. "I'll figure it out."

"Maybe"—she suggested—"there was a reason for that accident today, so you could be here for Malcolm and for Lily. You are on vacation, after all."

"I don't believe in cosmic machinations, Eve. But I'm here and you're right. The timing is good. I'll bring her home tonight and then we'll take it from there."

Eve turned back to the child. "She might freak out to wake up at your place tomorrow, not knowing you. At least she and I made friends tonight. Maybe I should come with you. I could stay on your couch. Then I can introduce you in the morning. I've got some work scheduled on the Christmas Ball later in the morning, but, until then…"

He couldn't help the relief that flooded his expression. "Really? You wouldn't mind?"

"Not at all. It's almost midnight. Neither one of us is

going to get much sleep anyway."

Before he could think better of it, he grabbed her in a hug. "Thank you."

After a moment of surprise, she hugged him back. But the soft press of her breasts against his chest, the sweet smell of her hair… even how small she felt in his arms, made him suddenly aware of what a tactical error it had been to get this close.

Backing away, he mumbled, "I'll just…" Eve nodded as he jerked a thumb at Lily then moved over to pick her up, cradling the little girl in his arms. She cuddled against his chest, sound asleep.

For a moment, he froze in his tracks, looking down at her. Something inside him arched toward that feeling. The feeling of a child, safe in his arms and a woman like Eve standing beside him.

"You okay?" Eve asked with a curious look.

He banished the feeling as soon as it occurred. *No time for that. Remember where you're going.* "Yeah. Fine. Let's go."

With a tip of his chin, he gestured for Eve to follow him and together, they headed toward his car.

THREE HOURS LATER, Eve lay awake, staring at the dark ceiling of Ben's bedroom. He'd insisted on giving her his bed to share with Lily, while he slept on the couch. She'd wanted to fight him on it, but it was futile. Exhaustion was a given for them all, but now, with Lily sleeping beside her, Eve allowed the repeat of the last disaster of a day to replay in her head over and over—the car accident, the news about Malcolm, the awkward hug in the waiting room, Patsy's family in chaos again.

What a mess.

Obviously, she had cancelled dinner with her parents and forbade them to worry or come to the hospital. But her stepmom, Jaycee, had no sooner hung up than she called Eve's sister, Kate, who had promptly shown up in the hospital waiting room for an hour or so for moral support.

"The day was an unmitigated disaster," Eve had said when prodded to come clean. "And it was totally my fault."

"I blame the reindeer," Kate replied. "But you're both okay, that's all that matters."

"But I ruined his vacation. And if I hadn't been distracted by his thigh—"

"Wait. His thigh?"

"You say that like you have no idea what I'm talking about. Have you seen his thighs?"

Kate shrugged. "I will admit, Dr. *Mc*Tyler is… quite attractive, but I have mostly stopped noticing thighs on men other than Finn. Because, well… the bull rider thing. Oh, and his forearms. Those are hot, too. Actually," she went on, "just about everything about him is—"

"We were talking about Ben."

"Oh. Sorry. Ben. So… his thigh?"

"*Yes.* I didn't tell him this, of course, but I was glancing at it. I mean it was right there—all flexed and everything and, well, I was distracted. And then, suddenly, there was this reindeer."

Kate tutted. "Hmm. Ogling while driving… it's a dangerous thing. But I thought you two were just friends."

Eve petted Lily's hair as she lay asleep in her lap. "We are. But that doesn't mean—"

"That you're not hot for him?"

"That I don't wish things could be… different."

"Ahhh," Kate said. "Now we're getting somewhere. Different how?"

"More," she explained, "than friendship."

Kate sent her a sympathetic look. "Lots of great relationships start with friendship. I mean, from what I understand. I wouldn't know personally."

Eve chuckled. The only man who had ever meant anything to Kate was Finn, and their relationship had started out as anything but friendly. Or platonic.

"Is he dating someone else?" Kate asked.

"Aside from every nurse in this facility throwing their coins at his fountain, I don't think so. But do you know what he told me tonight? He hates being in Marietta for Christmas. Actually, he's not a fan of the holiday. That's why he booked this trip. Seriously, who hates Christmas?"

"Not everyone is as Mary Poppins about Christmas as you, Evie, for lots of complicated reasons. I don't know Ben that well, but Jake does. And from what he's told me, Ben's childhood was not all puppy dog tails and rainbows. And that may involve a certain time of year many people have issues with. Look, if Christmas isn't your thing, Marietta in December can be like fingernails on a chalkboard."

Now, lying in his bed, Eve pondered how much she really knew about him, despite their friendship. He rarely talked about his family, who'd moved away from Paradise Valley when he'd started college. His father had been a surgeon, too. That much she knew. His mother, some society page woman was all she'd heard. But the fact he had plans to see neither one of them over the holidays was telling enough.

She tugged the covers up to her chin and inhaled his lingering scent with an uneasy sigh. How many times over the past year had she'd imagined this moment? Her, lying right here in his bed? Too many. But to be fair, her fantasies had never included a four-year old, snoring softly beside her, and Ben curled up alone on the couch in the next room.

And was the sudden weirdness between them a direct result of the accident? Or was it something else? Granted, they had some tacit agreement about their friendship and how they wouldn't venture beyond whatever was between them. Whatever *that* was.

Actually, she couldn't remember agreeing to that. But apparently he had. *But things naturally evolve, don't they?* Progress? Usually. Still, today made her wonder if she wasn't just chasing smoke, or pining after a man who didn't—*and would never*—want her.

Eve tossed and rolled over, staring out the dark window at the stars.

He was a scientist, a pragmatist. *I don't believe in cosmic machinations, Eve.*

Oh, but she did. She believed there was no such thing as coincidence. Or even accidents. She believed in destiny, soul mates, and love at first sight. Things happened for a reason and, most times, that reason remained invisible until a long way down the road.

She believed Malcolm and Lily had been the fortunate recipients of such today, whether Ben wanted to admit it or not. And now, thanks to an escaped reindeer, they were all stuck in the very same cosmic machination.

Chapter Two

"I WANT MY daddy."

Ben jerked upright on the too-soft sofa and blinked awake, his focus slow to sharpen. From the half-darkness outside his window, he guessed it couldn't be later than six a.m.

Standing less than a foot away from him, Lily stared at him as an alien child might a human being—with big-eyed skepticism.

So much for their plan to make introductions first thing.

He ran a hand down his face and glanced toward the bedroom, hoping to see Eve coming to his rescue. No such luck. He ached all over, but he couldn't be certain if it was from sleeping on the couch or from the car accident yesterday.

"Morning," he said to the child.

"I want my daddy." She repeated a little more urgently, twirling a long, fancy white feather between her fingers.

"Right. Perfectly understandable." Without breaking eye contact, he shouted at the other room, "*Eve*?" Silence. To

Lily, he said, "Your daddy's taking a little rest in the hospital but you'll see him later. I promise."

She blinked at him, expressionless, but for the quiver in her lower lip.

"No, really," he said. "We'll go see him today."

Emotion balled up behind her eyes. "No. Right now."

He shoved a hand through his sleep-challenged hair. "Uh… *Eve*?"

She appeared at the doorway of his bedroom, stumbling to a stop as she tugged the extra-long tee shirt he'd given her to sleep in down her sweetly shaped thighs.

Her gaze landed on his bare chest then jerked back to his face. "Hi."

"Hi." He pointed to the girl as if somehow, magically, Eve could make this problem disappear. "Lily's up."

The little girl's gaze flicked expectantly to Eve.

"Hi, Lily. Remember me from last night?"

Lily nodded.

"And this is Ben. And this is Ben's house. He's a friend of your daddy's and also his doctor. He's helping Daddy to feel better."

Ben stood, wrapping his blanket around his waist. "You probably don't remember me, but we've met before. When you were littler." She tilted her head back and gave him that alien child-look again. "It's been a while."

He'd repeatedly called Malcolm after Patsy's death to meet him for a drink or a meal, but Malcolm had politely declined, using Lily as his excuse. Work got busy and Ben hadn't called for months. Only now did he realize what a bad friend he'd been to both.

"You must be so hungry this morning," Eve said to her. "I am."

"Do you have any bananas?" Lily asked.

"Nope," Ben said, suddenly picturing his pathetically bare cupboards. He usually just ate at the hospital. He practically lived there anyway.

"Waffles?" she asked.

"No." He sent Eve a desperate look.

"Strawberries? Peanut butter? Nutella?"

To each question, he shook his head as he sidled closer to Eve. "She's very verbal for four."

She tilted an amused look at him. "That happens."

"What *do* you have?" Lily asked.

Ben scratched his bare chest. "Coffee creamer?"

"Hey, I have a good idea," Eve said brightly. "Let's all go to breakfast!"

THE MAIN STREET Diner opened early and they were not the first to slide into a booth there. As he expected, the restaurant was decked out for the holidays with evergreen garlands, twinkling with little white lights on the walls and three small Christmas trees flocked with snow and red bulbs placed around the diner. On every table sat a mason jar filled with rock salt, cranberries and a candle, festooned with local greenery. Everywhere Ben landed his gaze, there was the holiday in all its shimmery glory.

Coffee promptly appeared before both of them, along with a small glass of milk for Lily. Sally, the waitress, seemed to know Lily, making small talk with the child and giving her crayons to draw with even as the white ball from the waitress's Santa hat dangled between them.

"Where's your daddy today?" Sally asked the child.

"He falled off the ladder and broke his leg," Lily straightened her white feather at a perfect right angle to her coloring paper. "He didn't cry, but I did."

Sally shot an alarmed look at them. In her late forties, Sally had the face of a woman who was no stranger to heartache, with lines prematurely grooved around her eyes and cheeks. But despite her hard life, she was nearly always smiling when Ben saw her here.

"Oh, no. Maybe he needs that feather more'n you right now, darlin'."

Lily stopped coloring for a moment, considering that.

Strange thing to say. Ben's gaze sharpened on the feather lying beside her drawing. She hadn't let it out of her sight since he'd first laid eyes on her.

"I take it you two know each other, Sally?" Eve asked.

"Sure do. Lily and her daddy come in here regular. He'll be all right?"

"He's going to be fine," Eve answered. "We're going to

see him after breakfast, aren't we, Lily? He'll just be in the hospital a little while."

"Over Christmas?" Sally tsked.

"Probably so," Ben admitted quietly.

"Oh. Well, that's a darned shame. Because… well, she went to all that trouble."

Eve frowned. "I'm sorry, what?"

"It was all planned out." Sally tucked her pencil behind her ear. "She left nothin' to chance."

Ben intervened in the confusion. "Who?"

Sally glanced down at Lily and mouthed '*her mama*.'

Eve exchanged looks with him, suddenly sure Sally had her facts confused, since Patsy had been gone almost a year. She must be thinking about another family in town. But neither of them were about to correct her in front of Lily.

Eve said, "Okay, Sally, I think Lily would like some silver dollar pancakes, isn't that right, Lily?"

Engrossed in her crayon drawing, she nodded. "Banana, please."

"Oh, isn't she polite? You got it, darlin'. And what can I get for you two?"

"Just the coffee for me, thanks." Ben lifted his mug.

"Veggie omelet, please." Eve handed her back the menus, wrapped her hands around her coffee mug and looked at Ben as Sally headed back to the kitchen. "You should eat. You haven't had a decent meal since yesterday morning."

The chill from outside was just beginning to leave his

hands as he wrapped them around his own coffee mug. He grinned at Eve. "Worried about me?"

"Just looking out for you, is all. I figure I owe you at least one good meal after yesterday's disaster."

"I might just take you up on that after we get this all straightened out." Before he could interpret the expression that crossed her face, his cell rang and he glanced down at the caller ID. "I'm sorry, I have to take this. Will you two excuse me for a minute?"

"Of course." Eve leaned closer to Lily, picked up a blue crayon and began drawing a tic-tack-toe grid. "Ever play this game?"

Ben answered his cell as he walked toward the restrooms at the back of the diner. "Dr. Camran? Yes, of course, *Angus*. I guess you got my message last night. I'm so sorry."

Doctor Angus Camran, a highly respected craniofacial surgeon with roots in Scotland, sounded far away, which he, indeed, was. Poised at the edge of the Honduran jungles, Camran and his team of specialists were about to embark on a medical mission into the remotest villages of Central America. Without him.

"'Course, to say we're disappointed," Camran began, in his thick brogue, "hardly covers it. But relieved t' hear ye weren't hurt in the accident."

"I'm disappointed, too, sir. I was really looking forward to the next two weeks."

"I wish we could wait for you here, but we canna. Too

many cogs in the movin' wheel, as it were. But, as you're aware, this trip—your part of it, anyway, was for your own peace of mind, not ours, and t' straighten out any misgivin's you might have about our offer. See how you felt about how you fit in. We know we want you on our permanent team. That decision's purely yours, o'course. The need is great and you'd be a marvelous asset to us down here."

"That's good to hear, Angus, but—"

"And," Camran went on, "t' be honest, it'd be a shame to delay your decision for another few months until our other team is ready t' go, or when you can manage more time off. Your skills are quite in demand as you might imagine, doctor."

He'd spent many a night lying awake, imagining the kinds of complicated cases he'd encounter down there—the challenges, the experience. But if he was being honest, he felt incomplete here. Unfulfilled. He'd never actually aspired to be his father, the fabulous surgeon who rode on the coattails of his reputation his entire life and never did a damn altruistic thing for anyone. His father's life—while ostensibly about medicine, was all front and no back. No heart. And if there was one thing Ben wanted to insert into his life's calling, it was… meaning. He just couldn't figure out how to do that here. And if it was—to some degree—a "*geographic*," then so be it. Perhaps the old adage about never going home again was true because lately, all he could think about was leaving.

"I think we can both assume that I would enjoy the challenge down there, Angus. I don't see me getting time off again anytime soon and I know you're pressured for an answer." He bit back any misgivings that still lingered. "So, if you'll have me, I'd love to join you. So… yes."

He heard Camran give a muffled whoop. "Fantastic! We couldn't be more thrilled. O' course you'll need a bit 'o lead time and give your notice there, but how soon do you think you could make it down here?"

"That depends on the hospital here. And a small"—*four-year-old*—"complication that's come up. But I'll let you know as soon as my ducks are in a row. Definitely after the first of the year."

Ben wrapped up his call with a thrill chasing through his blood he hadn't felt in a long time. He hadn't planned on saying yes today. But it was done. Now maybe he could endure Christmas here, with Honduras waiting on the other side. No reindeers in the rainforest. Nor—he glanced up from his phone to see Eve and Lily with their heads together over her drawing—women like Eve to remind him of what he couldn't get it together to have.

AT THE HOSPITAL a half hour later, while Nurse Kelly Reynolds sat outside with Lily, Ben and Eve entered Malcolm Sherman's room. Ben wanted to be sure that seeing her father wouldn't be too much of a shock for Lily after everything he'd been through yesterday. And Eve refused to be left behind.

Malcolm flicked a smile at them as they entered. As if the past year hadn't already been hard enough on him, this accident had put the proverbial cherry on top of a terrible time in his life. Except, apparently for the occasional forays to the Main Street Diner, he'd spent the year holed up with Lily on the ranch he and Patsy had shared. Now this.

"Ben? Eve?"

Eve bent down and kissed his cheek, teasing, "Malcolm, you look like you fell off a ladder."

Malcolm smiled weakly. "I *feel* like I fell off a ladder. Where's Lily? Is she okay?"

Eve took his good hand in hers. "She's fine. She's outside with a darling nurse named Kelly. Ben wanted a look at you first. I was here last night when you arrived."

Ben walked around the bed to his other side. "Eve stayed with Lily in the waiting room until I was done piecing you back together and she slept at my place last night for Lily."

Malcolm lifted her hand and kissed her fingers. "Thank you. I can't tell you how much I appreciate you taking care of her. And Ben, I know that was a lot to ask but—" He started to sit up, but got dizzy and lay back down.

"Take it easy. That's what friends are for, right?"

Malcolm automatically reached for Ben's hand, but his right hand was in a cast and he winced at the sudden movement. "I haven't been much of a friend to you this last year. I haven't been much good to anyone."

"Mal—" Ben started to protest. "I'm the one who hasn't been the good friend. I should have called you more. Dragged you off that ranch of yours."

"You tried. I am the one who turned you down. But listen"—Malcolm insisted—"I've got to get out of here. I can't stay here for Christmas. I've got all the horses and a mare in foal and—"

"Your neighbor's covering you for now. Jonas Thomkins called in this morning and left a message at the nurse's station."

Malcolm squeezed his eyes shut in relief, but he and Ben knew that was only a temporary fix. He would be recuperating for a good long while and someone would have to take over his heavy chores. With a small ranch tucked away not far from Eve's parents' Lane's End, Malcolm bred and raised fine quarter horses not only for local ranchers, but to competitive quarter horse riders all over the country. It had been easy to lose himself in that work for the past year, but isolating himself out there hadn't been good for either him or his daughter.

"My neighbors…" Malcolm began, getting choked up. "I'm very lucky. But that's not the only reason I can't stay in the hospital. I really need to get out of here."

Ben flicked a look at Eve, who lowered her eyes. "You may be out of luck on that count. From what I understand, you could be in here almost a week. More if you don't take it easy."

"A week!" Malcolm's already pale face got ashen. "But you're my doctor. You can sign me out. They already had me up and walking last night."

Ben shook his head. "First, I wouldn't. Even if I were your doctor, which I'm not anymore, I'm not even technically back in the rotation for the next ten days. I happened to be here last night and I stepped in at the last minute for the on-call surgeon, Dr. Bennett, who was tied up in another surgery. But since I'm not on the schedule yet, he'll be overseeing your ortho treatment now. He's awesome, believe me. And Dr. Tillsworth—a top notch neurologist from Livingston, will be looking after that thick skull of yours."

Malcolm shook his head. "You don't understand. I can't be in here. I've got to do Patsy's Christmas. For Lily."

Patsy's Christmas? "Look, Christmas will happen with you in the hospital or not. If you need help shopping for Lily, I'm happy to—"

Malcolm gave a frustrated sigh. "You don't understand. She sent me a letter."

"Who did?" Eve asked. "Lily?"

"No," Malcolm said. "Patsy."

Exchanging another worried look with Eve, Ben lifted the chart at the end of the bed, scanning it for the latest results on his head CT.

"I know what you're thinking," Malcolm said with a frown. "It's not like that."

"Christmas is the last thing you should be worrying

about right now," Eve said to him. "You need to rest."

"No." Malcom pointed to the wardrobe where the clothes he'd been wearing when he was admitted were hung. "My coat. Please. Get me my coat."

Ben frowned, deciding to humor him instead of making things worse. They'd cut most everything but his jacket off of him, so it hung, lonely in the closet with his boots.

"It's the reason I was up there hanging lights," Malcolm said, pointing to an inner pocket. Ben pulled an envelope from his coat and started to hand it to him. But Malcolm brushed him off. "I'm still seeing double. Just… just read it. Eve can hear it, too."

Ben unfolded the letter skeptically. Maybe Malcolm had gone off the deep end. Patsy had been gone a year, so any letter she might have sent would be—

He scanned to the bottom of the page and there it was in red ink. "*I love you, now and forever, Patsy.*"

His gaze lifted to his friend, who was watching him closely. Ben felt his throat tighten. He'd loved Patsy like a sister since they were kids. Her death had nearly brought him to his knees. He could only imagine how Malcolm had survived it. But this… this didn't make any sense. He wondered if someone had played a sick joke on his old friend.

"Go on, read it," Malcolm said.

Ben cleared his throat and read…

Christmas, 2016

My Darling Malcolm,

If you're reading this letter, it means the doctors were right and I was overly optimistic. Not that I regret that one bit, as optimism got us this far, right? But all that's old news now, because Christmas 2016 is right around the corner. I know that because this letter will only be delivered if a) I'm gone and b) you're alone with Lily for the holiday. And, while I expected as much, I can hardly bear the thought of you two alone at Christmastime.

So, I'm taking matters into my own hands. Long distance, granted, but still, you know me. I can't help myself. I'm a meddler when it comes to my love for you and our daughter.

So here's the deal, darling. This letter was mailed by a friend a few days ago. It's the first of six envelopes you'll receive. But they won't come in the mail. They'll be hand delivered. And inside each one is something I want you to do with Lily. Something we would have done together. You see, I've enlisted some more friends to help me. Everyone knows their part and they've all agreed.

Now, Malcolm, I know you'd rather not, and I suspect you're spending altogether too much time shut up on the ranch when you're not taking care of our daughter. But, my love, Lily's still so little and she still believes in Santa Claus and Christmas and magic… and I don't want her to stop just yet.

So first thing, go find the Christmas lights up in the attic that I know you're ignoring and put them up. Lily needs to see them because they're happy. And you know how I loved our Christmas decorations. Oh, and don't forget the reindeer."

Ben flicked a quick, disbelieving look at Eve, who sent him a wide-eyed look back at him. He read on…

"Please humor me, will you, sweetheart? Play along? Promise? Think of me and I'll be thinking of you. Merry Christmas, my darling.

I love you, now and forever,
Patsy

P.S. Next stop, Sage's Copper Mountain Chocolates. Sage will know why you're there.

A muscle clenched in Ben's jaw as he slowly folded the letter and replaced it in the envelope.

Eve blinked at the suspicious moisture in her eyes. "Oh, Patsy…"

Ben cleared his throat. It was so like Patsy to do this. He'd known her since grade school. She was the girl every other girl wanted to be and the one every boy wanted to be with. He'd be the first to admit, he'd been one of those boys and his lifelong crush on Patsy had only taken a second seat to medicine and Malcolm—whom she'd fallen for and married after college.

When Ben had returned to Marietta after medical school to practice, she'd pulled him back into her wide circle of friends. She'd been a nut for Christmas and had taken great joy in decorating her home to the nines. He remembered one Christmas party at their house where no niche was ignored as a potential nest for holiday cheer, including the doorways, hung strategically with mistletoe. Playfully, she'd urged every party guest to find someone to kiss under the miniature shrub and delighted when they actually did. Inevitably, she'd wrangled her husband under each and every one to catch a kiss of her own.

The memory made him look away from Malcolm, who was watching him, his eyes full of memories, too.

"So..." Ben began, handing the letter to Malcolm, "Christmas lights, huh?"

He laughed and ran his good hand through his rough hair. "Yeah. You think she meant for me to hire someone to hang them?"

"I bet now she does," Ben said.

"God, she'd laugh if she could see me now."

Ben grinned, because he knew what Malcolm meant. Patsy had a way of making even the direst situations funny.

Malcolm looked off toward the window. "She never asked much of me, you know? Even at the end. She knew me well. And she knew I could never say no to her. So this thing she wants me to do, I have to do it. For Lily's sake. Because she was right. I didn't want to do Christmas this year. It was too soon. And because Lily's so young, I thought she wouldn't even miss it. But Patsy's letter… I realized I was wrong. I can't hide out from all the things Lily and I will have to do alone for the rest of our lives, can I? But now, I'm stuck here and—"

"We'll do it for you," Eve blurted without even looking at Ben. "Whatever it is Patsy wanted for Lily, Ben and I can handle it. Can't we, Ben?" Risking a look at him, she said, "You're on vacation, right?"

His fleeting fantasy of getting back to work and finding someone else to take care of Lily faded in the wake of Patsy's letter. He'd already let Malcolm down this year as a friend. Him and Patsy both. Helping with Lily now seemed the least he could do. And he *was* on vacation. Technically.

"I—" he began, fumbling with the chart in his hands. "Sure. Of course. We can definitely do that."

Eve turned her wide, open smile on him that felt like sunshine, and the twist of guilt he felt at having to be buffaloed into doing the right thing screwed a little deeper.

Relief colored Malcolm's expression. "Thank you, guys. That's… really? I'm so grateful. I'm sure you two are both so busy with your own lives and work…"

"Don't you worry about a thing," Eve said. "Lily will have a great Christmas this year. We'll make sure of it. You've come to the right place. I mean"—she grabbed Ben by the arm and pulled him closer to Malcolm—"you're looking at Saint Nick with a stethoscope here, Mr. Christmas himself. Why, there's nothing he likes more than holiday time in Marietta." She fluttered her lashes at him. "Isn't that right, Ben?"

The look he sent back to her was fraught with irony. "She's got me there, Mal."

"See?" Eve patted his arm. "So, I'll go get Lily and you two can have a quick visit and then you can concentrate on getting well quickly and coming back home."

Malcolm gave a wan smile and nodded as she disappeared out the door to his room, leaving Ben and him drifting into an awkward silence as Ben contemplated all that promise entailed.

Finally, Malcolm said, "Are you sure about this, Ben? Because if you can't—"

"No. I'm sure, man. Totally sure. I'm happy to do it for you." But even as he spoke he backpedaled toward the door.

"If you wanted to, you could stay out at my ranch," Malcolm said. "There's more room there and it might just be easier on Lily to be home. She has her toys and things that would make it easier on you. And you could keep an eye on my mare."

Ben stopped, his hand on the door handle. Spending a week under the same roof with Eve was a bad idea. A very bad idea. Because, as he pictured her in his tee shirt, standing by his bedroom door this morning, a hot stab of desire curled unexpectedly through him.

He rubbed his chest, the spot that still ached from its impact with the air bag yesterday. "Eve and I"—he hedged—"you know, we're not—"

"Together? I know. I'm not sure why not, frankly, but that's between the two of you. There's a guest room. Also there's Toby."

Ben canted a look at him. "Toby?"

"The cat."

Oh, yes. Now he remembered Toby—a grey and white striped behemoth of a feline who strutted around their place like Scar from *The Lion King*, prowling for victims.

Ben wasn't a cat person. Now dogs… Dogs, he could do, but cats?

"Let me run that idea by Eve. Would you… excuse me for just a second?"

EVE LOOKED UP at Ben's approach to the nurse's desk where Lily was sitting, perched on the counter. His expression reminded her of a thunderhead.

"We need to talk."

"Okay, but—"

He nodded to Nurse Kelly and the five other nurses surrounding Lily before steering Eve away from her down the hall. They stopped beside a crash cart parked in the hallway.

"That was pretty smooth, Canaday," he said in a voice too low to be overheard.

"I don't know what you mean," she said, blinking up at him.

"A pretty good end run."

She tilted a look at him. "Are you saying you don't want to help him?"

"No. I'm not saying that."

"No one is forcing you to go back. You're on vacation. However, I have it on good authority that after our little mishap yesterday, there was an actual pool betting against your taking time off."

"What?"

"Don't ask me. Ask them." She pointed to the gathering of nurses hovering near Nurse Kelly down the hall and staring his way.

He sent the ladies a cautious chin tip. Jessie Rodriguez, the newest nurse on the floor rolled her eyes and forked over a ten to one of the other nurses who gleefully pocketed it.

"Hey, I can take time off," he told Eve, sounding defensive.

"So… *do*," Eve dared.

"I'd planned to do just that before I was sidelined by a reindeer." With his arms folded, he shifted his backside against the crash cart, staring out over her shoulder.

Her face heated again. "I—again, I am sorry. Truly. And you could say no to him. To Lily. To Patsy, perhaps most of all."

He shoved a hand through his dark hair.

"But if you'd rather not, then I guess you'll have to take time off with the rest of us Whos here in Whoville"—she glanced back at Lily—"no matter how small." She fought not to grin as she said it.

"Ha. That's funny." His amused gaze roamed across her face as if he wanted to say something snarky. "Anyone ever mention that you're kinda pushy, Canaday?"

"Oh. Yeah. All the time. Ask my sisters."

With a sigh, he stared off over her head. "Okay. On two conditions."

This is progress. She lifted her eyebrows inquisitively.

"That royal '*we*' you used back there? As in '*we*' will make sure she has a great Christmas? I need a promise on that. I don't do Christmas and I have zero confidence I can do this on my own."

"Of course."

"And, second, Malcolm suggested we stay at his place with Lily. Which makes sense, since my place—"

"Feels a little like a hotel room?"

"Isn't childproof and her toys and bed and everything are there." A frown tugged at his mouth. "My place feels like a hotel room?"

She chuckled. "Sorry. I'm a stager by profession. The place could use a little personal touch, that's all. Some photos. Maybe some books that aren't medical journals and—" His words suddenly registered. "Wait. You said w*e?* *We* stay at Malcolm's? As in you and me? Together?" Her heartbeat picked up speed.

"Just until Malcolm gets out of the hospital. Don't worry. He has a guest room." Eve stuffed a ridiculous twinge of disappointment. "And also"—here, he paused dramatically—"there's a cat."

"I happen to love cats." *In fact, I might become a cat lady someday soon. Just me and my dozen or so cats, roaming around my lonely, spinster apartment in—*

"Good. Then you're in charge."

Eve bit her lip, then forced a smile. "I suppose that does make sense. All right. Done. But since we're laying down conditions, I have one of my own."

He grinned. "I'm not sure that you're actually in a position to bargain, considering."

"Nevertheless." She insisted.

"Okay, name it."

"Since you mentioned the royal '*we*,' you might recall that I'm doing the staging for the Graff Hotel Christmas Ball that the Daughters of Montana are putting on in a few days. And the prince who's taken over the top floor of the hotel will be attending?"

"Vaguely," he admitted, his eyes watching her twirl a strand of dark hair around one finger.

Instantly she dropped the strand. "Well… the event is coming up in three days. Much of the work is already done and, while I have a whole team backing me up, I won't be around for you and Lily the day of the ball, particularly. You know… last minute tweaks."

"I'm sure it will be amazing if you're doing it. Okay. Agreed."

"That's not the condition." He tipped a suspicious look at her and moisture sprang to her palms. "First," she said, "do you… have a tuxedo?"

"Tuxedo?" He repeated warily. "I… might."

"Good, because there isn't time to rent one. Okay, here it is. I… um… don't have a date," she said. "This is kind of embarrassing, since I'm expected to make an appearance. So that's my condition. Take me to the ball and we'll call it even. My parents will happily babysit for Lily, I'm sure, unless they're going. And in that case, we can find a sitter. It's only one night."

"Why no date?" he asked in all seriousness.

Eve studied a crooked linoleum square at the center of the floor. *Because my first—and only—choice was supposed to be deep sea diving in the Caribbean.* "I guess I just never got around to making that happen. Too busy, I suppose."

"Come on. You must have guys begging you for a date."

She shot a look at up him through her lashes. *Seriously, Ben?* "Throngs. But none of them happens to own a tuxedo." Impatiently, she asked, "So, can you take me or not?"

"Sure. Why not? I can do that, I guess."

On a groan, she pushed away from the crash cart, heading back to the nurse's station. "Try to contain your enthusiasm."

He followed her. "I mean, I'd… I'd love to take you."

"Don't get carried away," she said without looking back.

"Eve—wait." Ben grabbed her arm before she could reach the nurses' station. "That came out wrong. I'm sorry, okay? I'd love to take you. I'm just not really a 'ball' kind of guy. So you'll have to bear with me. I don't even dance. I mean, I'd like to dance with you, but…" He got an *ah-hell, someone-just-hand-me-a-shovel* look on his face.

"Relax," she said, "I just need an escort, Ben, so I don't look like an idiot showing up alone. If you don't want to dance with me, you certainly don't have to."

"No… it's not that I don't want to—" The pager on his belt went off and he grabbed it up like a man clutching a life vest in the open water. "I'd better take this. We'll talk later, okay?"

"Sure. Why not? I can do that, I guess." She left him standing there, as she gathered up Lily and walked her in to see her father.

Naturally, the nurses were all pretending they had heard nothing, but immediately broke up their little coffee clutch to get back to work. He pivoted on his heel and headed to the elevators.

He was the idiot.

The out-of-practice, say-everything-wrong idiot.

He jammed the first floor button on the elevator and took a step back. Why hadn't he just graciously accepted, like a normal man? He hadn't meant to hurt her feelings.

Idiot.

Stepping back from feelings was something that came naturally to him as a doctor. Something imperative to survival. But that wasn't how the rest of the world operated. He had only to look into Eve Canaday's beautiful eyes to see that she wore her feelings on her sleeve and if he was going to do this thing with Lily and Eve, he'd better damn well be careful around that.

Just as the elevator was about to slide shut, a slender, female hand caught the steel doors and popped them open. The tall brunette wearing an exquisitely tailored grey suit with a tight pencil skirt slipped in beside him with a grin.

"Hi, there, handsome."

Kimberly Trask. Laxco Pharmaceutical rep extraordinaire. He was definitely not in the mood for her right now. "Hey, Kimberly."

"What are you doing here?" she asked. "I thought you were going on vacation."

"I was. I had a little mishap on the way to the airport."

"Mishap? Oh, no. Is that where you got that sexy little"—she reached up to touch his lip before he could duck away—"cut on your lip?"

He grabbed her hand and delivered it back into her own space. "Yeah. But I'm fine."

"Bet you can't guess where I've just spent the last two weeks."

Had she been gone two weeks? He hadn't even noticed.

"Nope. Where?"

"Greece. On a cruise. A sailing cruise. You know, one of those tall ships?"

Ahh. Greece... Or Roatan. Or Timbuktu. Anywhere sounded better than here right now.

She gave him a sexy shoulder bump. "You should've come with me. Maybe next time."

Because clearly, she hadn't taken this voyage alone. Kimberly had the body of a Victoria's Secret model and the instincts of a shark. But she did have a certain charm and ambitions that went far beyond pharmaceutical sales, including flirting with most of the eligible doctors here. And some who were not so eligible. He'd taken her out once to dinner, but he'd never slept with her. She had designs on him. Even he could see that. But he wasn't interested.

"I'm serious," she said. "You should come."

"Your boss would be scandalized," he said, trying to put her off, but his mind turned back to Eve and the look on her face as she'd walked away from him.

"My boss would *pay,*" Kimberly countered, tucking her arm into his. "It'd be fun. Just you, me, and all that turquoise water?"

He just smiled noncommittally up at the elevator lights and disconnected himself from her as they slowly made their way to the first floor. He'd have to talk to maintenance about speeding up these damned things. Finally, the bell dinged and the doors slid open.

"Hey—" She grabbed his hand before he could get through the doors. "Since you're in town, how about taking me to the Christmas Ball this weekend? I'm dying to go and I don't have a date," she said with a pout.

He hadn't imagined he'd be grateful for Eve's invitation, but suddenly, he was. "I'm sorry, I can't. I'm taking a friend."

Her expression dipped with disappointment and she teased, "A friend? Should I be jealous?"

Jealous of Eve? It surprised him to think, *hell, yes, in every way possible.* The gorgeous, accomplished, ambitious pharma rep should be jealous of Eve, who was everything Kimberly was not without even trying. Adorable, funny, smart, and unpretentious.

But astonishingly, he'd never really thought of her as anything but… just Eve. For good reason, he reminded himself. He'd spent the last year hoping not to screw up a good friendship with her by complicating it with feelings that would only get him into trouble. And now, with his exit from Marietta looming, he felt all the more certain that acting on any impulses he had about her would only end badly. For both of them.

But he gratefully avoided answering Kimberly's question when the pager on his hip buzzed the second time. He held up his hands in a helpless gesture. "Gotta run, Kimberly. See you later."

She sent him a pouty smile and finger waved goodbye.

Five minutes later, he stood outside the chief of staff's door and took a deep breath before knocking.

Chapter Three

Eve, Ben, and Lily pulled into Malcolm's driveway, freshly plowed, courtesy of one of his kind neighbors down the road, who'd no doubt heard about Ben's accident. The ranch was close to Eve's parents' place and she knew it well. Malcolm's quarter horses were the envy of every cowboy in Marietta, but aspirational to most. They went for considerable money after Malcolm got through training them and he bred only the best.

The small herd hurried to the fence line as they pulled in, wearing their shaggy winter coats, no doubt hoping to see Malcolm. They were going to be disappointed. But Eve decided at least feeding them carrots would be a good activity for Lily. Eve had grown up around horses for most of her life and spending this week with them so close would feel like home.

The house was not a typical ranch house, but had the bones of a craftsman, which, over the years had been remodeled and updated with grey paint and burgundy trim. She'd always loved this place. Maybe it was because Patsy had made such a home of it, with the adorable window boxes in every shuttered window—which, in the summer, were always filled with glorious color. But now, it was blanketed in white, the latest snowfall covering the surrounding shrubs like plain white pillows.

She and Ben exchanged glances. He looked every bit as unsure about this whole thing as she felt. But maybe this was exactly what they needed. The universe had conspired to put them together here. By the end of their week, something would shake loose. She had already braced herself for worst because that's just what she did. But at least Lily would have a Christmas this year. If nothing else, they would make sure of that.

"This house doesn't look ready for Christmas at all," she said to Lily. "I think we should fix that, don't you?"

Lily nodded shyly.

"Do you want to help us?"

She nodded again. "Because Santa can't find it on Christmas without the lights."

Eve smoothed her blond hair back. "Oh, I wouldn't be too sure about that. Santa has his ways, just in case the lights don't get up in time. But just the same, we should make it easier on the old guy. Right, Ben?"

Lost in his own thoughts, he jerked a look back at them. "Hmm? Ah, right. Absolutely. Lights. I'll just bring in our things first." He walked up the steps and felt above the doorway for the key Malcolm had told them would be there, then, he went to the car for the bags they'd each hurriedly packed that were stowed in the trunk.

Inside, Toby, the cat assaulted them immediately, rubbing up against Ben's legs and meowing loudly. "Cat," he said to Eve, a one-word call for help.

"I'll feed him. I bet Lily knows just where his food is."

Toby—the grey tiger—was a tyrant, but a sweetheart and besides wanting attention, he wanted to eat. Once they'd soothed the beast, they headed back outside to find the ladder. It was stacked neatly at the side of the house.

Ben stared speculatively up at the second floor of the house from where Ben had fallen. "Do you think Santa would mind much if we kept the lights down on the porch? Maybe, just the bushes?"

"I think even Patsy would approve," Eve said. "Lily, you and I can put up the reindeer."

AN HOUR OR so later—grumbling aside—as the sun began its descent Ben plugged in the string of lights then stepped back with Eve and Lily to assess. If he did say so himself, his first attempt at stringing Christmas lights had turned out passably well. He'd outlined the porch roof and pillars and covered the snow-laden bushes with glittering twinkle lights.

Lily was ecstatic, clapping her mittened hands together and jumping up and down in the snow—the first hint of happiness he'd seen from the child.

"Look!" she cried. "The reindeer's alive!"

Indeed, one of the two willow reindeers' heads swung side to side as his nose blinked red.

"What shall we call him?" Eve asked. "He's got to have a name."

"Earl?" Ben suggested dryly.

Eve bit her lips and shot him a questioning look.

Ben shrugged with a wink. "He reminds me of a used car dealer's sign I used to live near in medical school. '*Earl's Pearls—Pre-Owned Cars with Pedigrees.*'"

"How about Katy?" Lily suggested, not swayed by Ben's idea.

With the ever-present feather in her hand, she swiped it through the air like a magic wand, dubbing the reindeer Katy.

"Oh, it's a girl?" With pointed look at Ben, who tacitly withdrew his suggestion, Eve bent down to Lily's level. "I think that's a perfect name."

"I know," Lily said with the supreme confidence of a four-year-old.

Ben fist pumped in the cold late afternoon air. "Girl power."

"That's right, huh, Lily?" Eve gave a fist pump, too.

Lily got the joke and giggled. Her cheeks were red with cold and her breath a steamy cloud of white.

"Who's hungry?" Eve asked. "I think it's time for dinner. Want to help me?"

Wide-eyed, Lily could hardly contain her enthusiasm as the two of them walked together into the house. Watching them go, Ben guessed Lily might hardly even recall cooking with her late mom, though he knew she had, often. Though he couldn't attest to it himself, cooking was one of those things moms did with their children, and Lily was no exception. He had no idea how much of her mom Lily even remembered at four. But she seemed to be getting more comfortable with Eve and, possibly, with him as well and if that made for an easier Christmas for the child, then he was all for it.

Snow began to fall, filtering down through pine trees bordering Malcolm's property, the red and green lights like twinkling flecks.

He shuffled his boots in the show, taking in the lights as the sky grew darker. 'Katy' bobbed her slender willow head at him, reminding him of all the Christmases he'd missed out on as a child while his parents went about their separate lives.

In particular, he remembered the year—he'd been around ten—when his parents had both been out of town for the holiday and he had ended up in the hospital with scarlet fever that had come on like a freight train and left him lying in bed with a nanny by his side. Two days later, his mother had swooped into town, but that hadn't been soon enough for him. He'd learned that day never to count on anyone but himself.

Looking in at Eve, though, he couldn't imagine her ever doing what his mother had done. No, she'd be the one holding the hand of the child who'd been ditched. Here she was, mothering Lily and all he could think was what was it about her that terrified him so much?

He shook off the thought.

Christmases past. Spilled milk and all that. And he surely wasn't the only one who simply managed to get through them by the numbers. Lily would have to do the holiday without her father mostly this year and that seemed particularly cruel, considering what she'd been through already. He owed it to her, or at least to Patsy, to figure out how to paint between the numbers, somehow, and make this Christmas one to remember.

This one, being his last one in Marietta for quite some time, it seemed the least he could do.

At the hospital, he'd told his chief of staff his decision about joining Camran's team. His chief had pushed back, naturally, wanting him to stay, but said he wouldn't stand in his way. He even suggested Ben take a temporary leave of absence from his position here to take the other job. Ben said he'd consider that. But a leave of absence felt more like a Band-Aid than a substantive change, which was what he needed. Yes, a new place, a new job, new challenges. That was what made life worth living.

Inside the house, he heard Lily squeal with laughter and he squinted at the frosted glass on the front window. Inside, the shadowy shapes of Eve and Lily dancing to some wacky holiday music playing in the background. A corner of his mouth lifted and he snapped a picture of them with his phone for Malcolm.

Of all the places he'd expected to find himself, here, fulfilling a little girl's late mother's wish list was the last one he could have imagined. Even more, doing all that with Eve Canaday.

He exhaled a steamy breath in the half-light of twilight.

Yet… there was something about her. Something that gave him pause as he stared in at the moving shadows inside the house like a child with his nose pressed against the glass of a shop filled with treats. That world, that intimate, belonging world, was not meant for men like him. Men who itched to travel and move and revise. It was for men like Malcolm who could love a woman with everything he had, even after she was gone. Personally, Ben had never known that kind of love. Ever.

Did love even exist for men like him? It seemed hardly worth pondering. He barely had time for the commitment he'd made here, much less muddying the field with pointless wishing.

The sound of a pickup truck pulling up the driveway—headlights illuminating the glittering snow—caught his attention. The pickup stopped half way up the drive and the driver waved at him.

"Dr. Tyler?"

Ben started toward him. "That's me."

The man reached a hand out the window. "I'm Malcolm's neighbor, Jonas Thomkins. I've been taking care of his horses for him." Jonas looked to be close to Ben's age, but had the rough and tumble look of a life lived outdoors.

A two-day growth of beard shadowed his jaw and his deep blue eyes seemed to be taking him in with an assessing look.

Ben said, "I'm sure Malcolm appreciates your help. I know I do. He's pretty fond of those horses."

"So am I," Jonas admitted. "Why don't you hop in and I'll drive us out to the barn. I'll introduce you to the girls."

Not about to turn down a warm ride down the five-hundred-yard snow packed lane, he hopped in.

As they rattled down the drive, the horses ran along the fence line as if playing a game with the truck, kicking up their heels in the snow. "I put them up for the night," Jonas said, "just to be safe. Even though they have access to the covered outdoor riding ring to get out of the snow, the temperatures are dipping this week and they're better off under full shelter." He pulled to a stop and swung out of the truck, grabbing an axe out of the back of the truck bed. Ben followed him to the oblong metal watering trough that was frozen over with a layer of ice.

"Here's the only thing you should keep an eye on between my stops." Raising the axe, he brought it down hard on the surface with a satisfying crack, and dispensed with the layer on top of the water. "Can't let it get too thick or they'll not only be thirsty, it'll damage the trough."

Ben nodded, following Jonas to the barn where he flipped on a light switch. Malcolm's barn was impressive, with a wide hallway down the center of two long rows of stalls and massive beams crisscrossed the area above it, open to the roof. On either side in the loft, hay bales stood stacked floor to ceiling in neat stacks. A small, brown bat, woken from sleep, fluttered over their heads for a moment before returning to the warmth of the rafters.

The smell of dried hay permeated the place along with the familiar horsey fragrance. He hadn't grown up owning horses, but he'd often found a way to borrow one to ride when he was a kid. Growing up in a ranch town like Marietta, where half the population were cowboys, he'd thought he wanted to be one, one day. But dreams shifted and mutated as one grew up. He still loved being around horses, though. Staying at Malcolm's gave him an unexpected bonus of rubbing shoulders with them again.

The fragrance of the barn almost instantly put him at ease. He and Jonas made quick work of filling each of the ten feed buckets with oats and the hanging mangers with flakes of alfalfa. Wordlessly, Ben pitched in filling the water buckets that hung beside the food. The stalls had been cleaned earlier and had a fresh layer of straw strewn across them. When they finished, the horses who were already waiting impatiently at the gate, hustled inside to their particular stalls, and Jonas latched them in. All except one.

"Have a look here, Doc."

Ben walked over to the stall closest to the front door. Inside, a very pregnant mare was already attacking her food. A beauty with a chestnut coat and black stockings, mane and tail, the mare flicked her ears forward at him.

"This here is Miranda. She's got a longer name that has something to do with a country song, but it's too much trouble to remember it." Jonas laughed. "She's only days… maybe a week away from giving birth, so she needs to be watched extra close. From tonight on, I planned on keeping her inside here so that foal stands a fighting chance in this cold. I'll be checking her morning and night, and feeding the others, but if you all want to keep your eyes open as well, it wouldn't hurt my feelings. Sometimes, these foals can surprise you. Make an unexpected entrance."

Ben ran a hand down Miranda's rounded side. He smiled to feel the roll of movement just under her skin and winked at Jonas. "I just felt the foal move."

Jonas grinned back. "Yup. Malcolm breeds his mares only to the best, strongest studs. That little one in there is already worth his weight. Here's my phone number," he said, handing Ben a business card. "Call me if anything happens. If she starts leaking milk, that's a pretty good sign something's about to start." Ben gave him his card in exchange. With all the horses buttoned up in the stable, Jonas said, "C'mon. I'll give you a ride back to the house."

Ben jumped back in the cab of the truck, out of the cold.

"I hear you're a bone doc," Jonas said, shifting the truck into gear and starting down the lane.

"Orthopedic surgeon."

Jonas whistled. "Bet this place feels like a whole different pond to you right now."

He rubbed a hand down his jaw. "Actually, I had a couple secret summer jobs in high school, mucking out stalls for a rancher I knew in exchange for letting me ride his horses. I kind of liked that work. Good for the soul."

"No kidding?"

"Nope."

Jonas nodded in approval. "Well, you'll do fine then. You and Lily. That little girl… she's a little warrior, that one. I'm not sure Malcolm would've made it through the past year if not for her. But then, that white feather of hers has pulled her through as well."

"I've noticed that feather. She holds onto it like its gold."

"To her, I guess it is. See it dropped out of the sky one day—probably some passing bird—but she got it in her head that it came off one of her mama's angel wings. And she won't let go of the thing." Jonas pulled up in front of the house. "Claims it's her mama's way of keeping her safe. And since Malcolm doesn't want to break her heart again, he lets her go on believing it."

A feather. From Patsy's angel wing. Ben slid a look out into the darkness behind the house. If ever there was someone who might drop a casual feather from her wing, it was Patsy.

"Why not?" he said. "She's only four. The feather is something to hold onto." *Be it a myth or a crutch.*

Jonas smiled. "I guess if it was my little girl, I'd do the same. But I don't have kids. Or a wife yet. So that's only a guess." He stuck his hand out to Ben. "Nice meeting you, Doc. You call, now, if you need anything. I'm just down the road a bit."

"Thanks. Nice meeting you, too. And thanks for your help."

"You bet."

"SHE'S FINALLY ASLEEP," Eve said later, returning downstairs with a plate of freshly made cookies she'd grabbed from the kitchen. "I think she's happy to be in her own bed again." Proffering the plate to him, she sank onto the leather couch opposite Ben, who had poured them both a glass of red wine and started a fire in the wood-burning fireplace. Toby luxuriated on the hearth as Jackson Brown's "Running on Empty" played low on the stereo. It did not surprise her that Ben had avoided Christmas music. "Cookie?"

"Don't mind if I do," he replied, snagging two.

Tiny sprinkles decorated the top of the messy, cut-out cookies she and Lily had made together—even he had cut out a few—and he licked a couple of sprinkles off his lip after he took his first bite.

"Mmm. You're good at this."

"At cookies? I think you actually made that one."

He reexamined the cookie, then gave it a nod. "Ah yes, the mutant Santa hat."

"Those are, um, bells."

"Of course they are. But I mean you're good at *this*," he said, gesturing with his cookie at the house. "Taking care of her. This place."

"Yeah? Well, don't get too comfortable. Tomorrow night it's your turn to read her stories, buster." A teasing grin stole over her face.

"That's fair." He took another bite. "And I always thought cookies came from a store. But these?" Examining the green and red sprinkles, he said, "These did not exist before you worked your magic in the kitchen. And presto-change-o."

He was teasing her, surely. She laughed and stuffed half a cookie in her mouth. "You say that as if you'd never decorated a Christmas cookie before."

"That's because I never have."

She swallowed. "Really?"

"Wasn't a priority in my house. Growing up, my mother wasn't exactly the 'cookie-baking' type."

"She worked?" Eve asked.

"Volunteered. Traveled a lot. She still sits on the boards of several hospitals and charities around the country. She never needed the money. The juice was acknowledgement for her."

This sounded like she needed another cookie. She took her time picking one from the plate. "And your dad, the heart surgeon? Did he travel, too?"

"Still does, actually. Teaches other surgeons his techniques all over the map."

"And… you?" she asked.

Ben frowned. "Me?"

"Yeah. Where did you fall in all this… traveling and volunteering?"

Brushing the cookie crumbs from his hands, he grinned and said, "Not making Christmas cookies."

"I'm serious, Ben. Who took care of you?"

"I was an only child. I had a series of nannies. And my parents weren't always gone. They were just… busy."

"I never knew that about you. I was a little younger than you and I never met either of them," Eve said, now feeling as if she hadn't missed anything. "But they left Marietta years ago, no? After you graduated high school? Your parents live in California now, don't they?"

"He does. She lives in New York City now."

"They're divorced?"

"No, that's too messy for her tastes. But that never stopped them from living apart. They always had separate lives. Now their marriage is just a formal bicoastal nonstarter."

The closeness of her own family—her two sisters and her father and stepmother, Jaycee, who'd married their widowed father when Eve was still young—was something she almost took for granted, though she'd have to have been raised in a cave not to realize her family was more an exception than a rule. Still, she had to remember to be more grateful.

"Do you see them much? Do they ever come back here?"

He took another, longer sip of wine as Jackson Brown sang about heartache, and for a moment, she feared she'd pried too deeply. "No," he said finally. "Not often. And Marietta, small as it is, requires too much maneuvering to get to. Now and then I'm summoned by my mother to attend some event with her, and my father makes it a point to see me at medical conferences when we intersect. But…"

"Oh, Ben…" She reached a hand over to him, pressing hers lightly atop his.

His blue eyes flicked up to hers and for just a moment, she glimpsed the hurt behind his admission. But an instant later, that, too, disappeared and he smiled the smile that had all the nurses sighing over him.

"It's no big deal. Really. They helped pay for my schooling. Inspired me to be a doctor. I love what I do and it's really thanks to them I get to do it." He squeezed her hand but didn't pull away.

It was, perhaps the first time, they'd actually held hands and Eve's heart pounded a little at his touch. If a man could have beautiful hands, Ben did. Long, graceful fingers, wide palms. His were not the calloused hands of the many cowboys hereabouts, but the smooth, skilled hands of a man who saved lives and limbs and dreams. She admired the hard work he'd done to get to where he was. The long years of schooling and practice. But somewhere in those intervening years, between his lonely childhood and now, his focus—except for his compulsion to run, even in the frigid, dead of winter—had narrowed to medicine alone.

Quite possibly, it was none of her business, but she believed a man like Ben needed balance. Like Malcolm did, whose life had thrown a wheel after Patsy and now limped along, incomplete and off-center.

But who was she to talk? Here she was, sitting on a couch beside the man she wanted and she was too scared to admit it to him. How screwed up was that?

"Somehow," she said, "I think you would have found a way to become a doctor on your own. It was your destiny."

"Maybe. Probably." His thumb rubbed across the top of her hand.

Toby, the tiger cat, chose that moment to leap onto the couch and settle his big self between them, breaking their momentary contact. Eve smiled and settled her fingers into Toby's fur behind his ears. Ben countered Toby by sliding away from him on the couch.

"He won't bite."

"Says you."

"Try it."

Toby purred and stared up at him with half-opened eyes as if Ben were a long lost lover. Cats never failed to choose the people who liked them least to reform.

Ben gave him a compulsory pat.

"I can't believe you never told me this before. About your family."

"Not my favorite topic."

"Hence, the bah-humbug dive trip to Roatan?"

He cleared his throat. "Right." And with that, he took another slug of wine. "Yeah, about that—"

She winced. "Sorry I brought it up. We won't go there. But it looks like you'll just have to put up with Lily and me for a little while."

"I can think of worse ways to spend my time." But he said it with a bit of a frown.

"Just think of this place as a vacation rental, complete with borrowed child."

"And a beautiful cookie maker."

Her turn to blush. "Yeah? Well, I'm more than just a cookie maker, I'll have you know."

"Reindeer dodger?" His grin was back.

"That, too. Plus, I make a mean snowball, if pushed, and, if you weren't averse to the ski hill, I'd show you my downhill skills."

"Who said I don't like skiing?"

"Orthopedic surgeon?" she said dryly. "In ski country?"

"I'll have you know I was competitive in high school.

Grand slalom events."

Eve sat back, surprised. "You are a wealth of secrets, Dr. Tyler."

Did she imagine it or did his gaze slide away from her when she said that?

"But, I don't actually ski anymore." He confessed, waggling his fingers at her. "Orthopedic surgeon. Gotta protect the hands."

With a laugh, she shook her head. "Ah. Well, maybe you'll still risk a snowball fight."

"Maybe."

Sometimes, when he looked at her the way he was just now, she wanted to kiss him. Just press her lips on his to see what happened. But she didn't. Couldn't. It would be too embarrassing if he balked.

But with the smell of the wood burning making her drowsy—or perhaps it was the wine, or the sugar crash from the copious cookies she'd consumed—she forgot herself enough to lean her head on his shoulder for a snuggle. His was a nice shoulder, sexy and firm and… snuggle-able.

For a few quiet minutes, they simply watched the fire flicker and snap, the smoke curling up the chimney.

"Hey, Eve," he said, a few minutes later, finally breaking the silence, "there's something I have to tell you."

Chapter Four

"HMM? WHAT?" SHE murmured. "Oh. I'm sorry. I just got sleepy." She rubbed her eyes. "Today's been a long day. Maybe we should hit the hay for the night." She sat up, blushing. "And by that, I didn't exactly mean hitting the hay, as in—oh, never mind."

He couldn't help but smile. Eve had a way of spinning his head around, making him lose his place. With her hair smelling like sunshine—some shampoo of hers he'd noticed before and her soft warmth, damn if his shoulder didn't feel suddenly bereft without her lying against him. He'd liked having her cuddle up to him. Which was why, naturally, he'd chosen that moment to spoil it with a confession. *Dumb ass move, Tyler. Dumb.*

"Did… did you say you wanted to tell me something?" she asked with a frown. She blinked at him expectantly.

"It was… actually…" He faltered.

He hadn't intended to bring this up tonight, so soon, but holding back seemed wrong the more they talked, and flat out lying would be the end result. Better to clear the air now and get it done with.

A smile bloomed on her face, making him forget the smile of any other woman he'd ever met. "Don't tell me. You were going to say you actually enjoyed hanging the Christmas lights."

How could a woman look so innocent and so gut-punch sexy at the same time? "I did enjoy it, actually," he told her. "But that's not it. I… haven't been completely honest with you."

She made a silly face. "About the skiing?"

"No. About Roatan."

Eve tilted a confused look at him. "What about Roatan?"

He took a deep breath. "I wasn't exactly heading there. I was really going to Honduras."

"Oh. O-kay. For… a dive trip?"

He swallowed thickly. "No. I was going on a medical mission of sorts into the jungle. It's an operation run by a Scottish doctor named Camran. He has a traveling team of doctors who go into remote, third-world places to treat people with no access to medical care."

"Well, that sounds amazing. But… wait. Why would you not tell me that?"

"It was supposed to be a trial run. An audition of sorts. Not for me, but for them. They wanted to hire me. Permanently." Ben pressed his palms together. "Actually… they *have* hired me. I've already given notice at the hospital. I'm… leaving Marietta."

She sat straight up and her face flushed a bright red. "Oh."

"I'm sorry," he said. "Sorry for not telling you the truth. I didn't want anyone to know until I'd decided. But after our little reindeer encounter, when the trip got cancelled, I knew it would be months before I'd get another chance to go and Camran wanted—needed—a commitment." Even to him, this excuse for lying to her sounded lame.

He watched her throat work as she distanced herself from him on the couch. "Oh." Her gaze landed on the table, the cookies. Anywhere, but his eyes. "Well. Congratulations. That's… wow. You've already quit? When do you leave?"

"After the first of the year."

"Ah," she said too quickly. "That soon."

He nodded.

"I don't guess I have to ask why. I mean, it's quite an opportunity. A challenge. And this is just Marietta, after all, a small, little speck on the backbone of the world, a town full of Whos breaking arms and twisting their ankles on ski slopes and on ranches." Her dark eyes glimmered but she smiled up at him quickly before shoving to her feet, busily brushing cookie crumbs from the coffee table and sweeping them into her hand. "Their gain, our loss. I'm sure it'll be great. But thanks for the heads up."

"Eve—" Getting to his feet, he knew he'd blown it.

Finally, she met his eye. "No, really, Ben. I'm… I'm happy for you. You'll be fantastic and brilliant, and they'll be lucky to have you." Then, with a dramatic yawn, she said, "But, gosh, I'm so tired. It's been a long day, right? I'm gonna just hit the—go to bed."

"Eve—" he pleaded again.

"See you in the morning?" she said with her back to him.

He nodded. "Sure."

"G'night."

"Night."

And with that, she was gone.

HOW HUMILIATING.

How ridiculous of her.

How many ways did he have to say no?

Eve flopped backwards down on her too large bed in the master suite—which Ben had insisted she take—arms spread wide as if somehow she could break her fall. Too late for that. She'd crashed and burned in extravagant flames and it was all she could do to not to cry over him. But tears gathered anyway.

Don't. He will never want you the way you want him. He practically spelled it out for you, just in case you missed it the last year or so.

Gawd! Curling up against him like a cat!

Which was probably why he told you then. Idiot. She swiped at her eyes.

Swallowing a curse, she knew she should just pack her bag and go. Just leave him here to be godfather to Lily all on his lonesome. After all, he lied.

But he didn't lead you on.

Yes, he did! Just exactly how did inviting her here for the week not feel like—

Eve shoved her hands through her hair.

No, he didn't. He'd been perfectly clear. He needed her. He never said anything about wanting her. And he never promised anything. Except a date to the ball.

Miserable, Eve sat up and buried her face in her hands. She never should have asked him. Not bad enough she'd go dateless to the damned thing. No, she had to bring a man who required a bribe to take her!

Yanking off her clothes, she tossed them onto her bed. She jerked on the nightshirt she'd packed, brushed her teeth, then crawled under the covers.

In the dark, she stared up at the ceiling. At least now she knew better than to delude herself into thinking they could be something more. He was leaving Marietta and that was that. He would go and she would stay and maybe they'd exchange emails now and then when he was somewhere within spitting distance to the internet. But those emails would grow less and less frequent until they stopped altogether and she and Ben lost touch. Because that was what happened when a person moved five-thousand miles away from another person and there was nothing but a fragile thread of a friendship holding them together.

Outside her window, stars spun in the black sky. The North Star, seemed to wink as she watched it, so bright among the others. *Starlight, star bright, first star I see tonight…*

She whispered, "Let him love me."

She remembered her niece, Caylee, asking about the practicality of wishes once, when throwing pennies in a fountain. "How come the wishes I wish don't come true?" And Eve had sagely told her, "Sometimes, the things we wish for are the things we have to work hardest for to make happen."

Blather.

That advice fell flat where Ben was concerned. No amount of work or wishing seemed destined to change his mind. Or help her sleep. So, she gave up on it and got up.

After washing her face, she stood in front of the bathroom mirror, trying to catch sight of the fatal flaw—the thing that made a man like Ben Tyler decide run all the way to Central America, rather than give her a shot. Was her nose too short? Freckles too many? Were her jokes not funny? Was she the kind of girl men never took seriously?

Maybe she should call Olivia, whose advice—in hindsight—she should have taken. But no. It was too late to call. And what would she say to her, anyway? *You were right? I should have made my feelings for him clear?*

Too late for that now.

Instead of calling her sister, she slapped on a headband and slathered on a mud mask she'd packed, which always made her feel better, and was just contemplating shaving her legs when she heard a soft knock at the door.

Eve froze and blinked at her reflection in the mirror. The mud was drying to a nice, horrid matte green.

“Eve? You still up?”

She waited. Hoping he’d go away. But he knocked again.

“Eve?”

“Um. Yes?”

“Can we talk?”

She set her jaw. “Sure. Go ahead.”

“Can you… will you open the door? I don’t want to wake Lily.”

She shook her head and took a deep breath. It would serve him right. She swept over to the door and swung it open.

The shocked look on his face was almost worth it. “Yes?” she asked with a tablespoon of sugar on top.

“*Oh.*” He backed up a step. “I didn’t realize you were—”

“A woman? Yes. As a matter of fact, I am. And women… like me… do masks now and then because we like to. They make us feel… good.” She nearly said “honest,” but decided that was too much. “Now, was there something?”

He scratched his thick, blond head. “Okay, so you’re mad at me.”

“No,” she said quickly. “I’m not.” *I’m mad at myself if you really want to know.*

Especially because she couldn’t help but notice he’d also changed into a tight, holey tee shirt and a pair of disintegrating sweats with a Stanford Medical School logo emblazoned across the hip which perfectly outlined his unfairly amazing physique.

"Yeah, you are." His gaze drifted downward to the peaks of her nipples jutting out from her nightshirt, before jerking his eyes back up again.

She wished some hole would open up in the floor and swallow her down it. Instead, her mud mask cracked.

"Okay," she admitted, her mouth half frozen in place with the mask. "Fine. I feel like a dupe. I drove you to the airport, Ben. Well, almost to the airport. Wrecked my car for you. And all that way, you let me think—"

"You're absolutely right."

"—that we were friends. At least I thought we were friends."

"We *are* friends."

She cast a longing look at her bathroom. "Huh. Last time I checked, friends don't lie to each other."

"I was wrong. Okay? You're absolutely—"

She held up an index finger. "I can't… Would you excuse me for a moment?"

Uncertain, he nodded and she walked with as much dignity as she could muster back to the sink to wash the mud off. A minute later, she returned toweling off her sparkling clean face.

"You were saying? Something about me being absolutely right?"

Leaning against the door jamb, arms uneasily folded, his mouth curved up into a grin. "That's right. You were."

The grin was throwing her off. "Anything else?"

"You look real pretty without makeup."

"Don't you try to butter me up, Doctor Tyler."

"Truth."

She yawned broadly.

"I'm serious."

"I'm not leaving if that's what you're worried about. If that's why you're still standing at my door, flicking compliments my way."

His gaze narrowed.

"A deal's a deal's a deal," she said. "I promised to help with Lily and I will. Besides, if you've decided the best thing for you to do with your life is run off to the jungles of Borneo or the Amazon or—"

"Honduras."

"Or Honduras, instead of staying in Marietta and facing whatever it is that's scaring you away, a place where people actually need and care about you, then who am I to try and stop you?"

He stiffened. "Scaring me? Nothing's scaring me away. I'm choosing to go. Of my own freewill."

A beat passed before she decided not to say what she wanted to say. "Okay. Whatever. Fine. I'm tired, Ben. I'm going to bed now. See you in the morning."

She started to shut the door, but he stopped it with his

hand, incidentally covering hers. His touch, as it always did, sent want curling through her. *Damn him!* She stared at his fingers for a long, gathering moment before meeting his blue, blue eyes.

And without any warning, he kissed her. On the mouth. A quick, buss of his lips that happened before she could evade it. Not that she would have. His lips were softer than she'd imagined and his kiss tasted of wine and desperation. Just a glimpse, yet she was sure she wasn't mistaken about the desperation.

And just when she thought he was done, he deepened the kiss, pulling her practically naked self against him. Her nipples grated against the fabric of her tee shirt, pressed up against the solid wall of his chest. She grabbed the door for balance, and then his shoulders, her breath catching in her throat. His tongue breeched the seam of her mouth and she opened to him, hungry for this taste of him.

His desire jutted against her hipbone, raw and hungry as her own. Her heart pounded and stars flickered behind her eyes. Kissing her. Ben was kissing her.

And then, almost as suddenly as that kiss had begun, he broke away, touching his forehead to hers before backing up to look at her.

His throat bobbed before he spoke. "Sorry."

"Are you?" she managed to say, feeling a gaping disappointment swell in the spot where only moments ago, hunger had been. "That kiss was an apology?"

"Yes. No." He shook his head slowly. "I don't know."

"Well, if you don't, I'm sure I don't either." Still shaken to the core from his kiss, she pulled the door between them.

"Thanks," he said, "for not leaving."

It was a moment before she could answer him. "You're welcome. But I'm… I'm doing it for Lily. That's what this is all about, after all. Right?"

He looked as if he wanted to say something more, but changed his mind. "G'night, Eve."

HOURS LATER, AS dawn broke over the field outside his window, Ben gave up on sleep and headed out to the barn. One by one, he let the horses—all but the pregnant mare—out of their stalls and into the snowy pasture. After cracking the ice off the surface of the watering trough, he spread a line of hay across the snowy field for the horses and headed back into the warmth of the barn. Stripping off his jacket, he got to work on the stalls.

The soothing scent of the hay calmed him as he shoveled manure into the wheelbarrow, routinely dumping it outside the barn in the compost pile, half-buried in snow. The work felt good—familiar—but his mind would not stop turning over what had happened between them last night.

The kiss.

What had he been thinking, kissing her that way? If it had begun as an apology, that intention had vanished the moment her lips had touched his.

He swallowed hard now, just remembering it. *Damn you, Tyler. What were you thinking?*

He couldn't stop thinking about the look in her eyes when he'd told her the truth. The one where she'd added up all the pieces of him and come up short. Who lied to a good friend that way? Why hadn't he taken her into his confidence? Why was he so afraid of admitting that it wasn't ambition driving him to try this new thing, but—*okay*—desperation? The need to feel… something… good about himself. To feel… whole? Meaningful. Something all the goodwill of Marietta could not seem to provide him? That maybe it was the dark hole inside of himself he'd found impossible to fill here? Because admitting that meant laying himself bare, and that he could not—would not—do.

So, he'd told her a half-truth. And he deserved her anger. Would she have helped him with Lily if he'd told her before she'd agreed to spend the week in this house with him? Probably not.

He rolled another wheelbarrow outside the barn and tipped it over, the straw and manure steaming in the cold morning air. At least he had a way to work off the tension arching between him and her. The cold shower had done him no good at all.

Her reaction last night, while it hadn't really surprised him, had caught him off guard, because while there had been anger—*expected*—there was something else as well—sadness.

Was it because he'd disappointed her, or because he was exiting their relationship as simply as he'd entered it, in a huge geographic to Central America?

The word relationship gave him pause. He meant friendship. That was what they had. Wasn't it? He'd kept his hands off Eve as much for her sake as his. He would only end up hurting her and the idea of doing that clawed at his gut. So why did he keep thinking how much he'd miss nights like that one, sitting by a fire beside her? Watching firelight illuminate her dark hair and flicker in her eyes. Her, making him laugh and him, revealing pieces of himself he couldn't seem to share with anyone else. Kissing her.

"*…instead of staying in Marietta and facing whatever it is that's scaring you away, a place where people actually need and care about you, then who am I to try and stop you?*"

The dark hole. That scared him. The never, ever filling it, that scared him.

Then another voice echoed in his head. His old man's oft repeated, "*If you know what's good for you, you'll save your heart for your work and avoid letting a woman tamper with it. She will only distract you from what's really important.*"

Ben squeezed his eyes shut. *Shut up, old man.*

Dammit, Eve *felt* important. And this week of putting his work on hold to take care of Patsy's daughter felt… important. So why did the advice of a man who'd lived his entire life aloof from everything but medicine—whose sexual dalliances with other women inevitably blew up in his face—

still rattle around inside Ben's head like an echo of truth?

He, alone, should decide what was true for him and what wasn't.

And when, by the way, had he let Eve Canaday get under his skin? Because she was there, dammit. She was the buzz in his head and the ache in his groin. The kiss last night had gotten away from him.

But more than sex—his only illusion of intimacy—he wanted a taste of a life he'd probably never risk trying to have. An intersection with something so unlike him that it might, somehow, brush off on him and leave him changed. Something Eve Canaday owned without even trying.

Something of which, selfishly, he wanted more.

But he didn't believe in miracles and it would take one to make him something he was not—a man who was enough for a woman like her. Something he had no business hoping for. He'd spent a big chunk of his life working for the approval of his disapproving father, the love of his distant mother, but somewhere along the line, he'd stopped all that and simply worked to be the best at what he did. That should be enough for any man who believed love was a fairy tale, shouldn't it?

He steered the wheelbarrow outside one last time and dumped it. From the corner of his eyes, in the fog-draped morning light, he caught a movement in the field to the east near the distant hedge of fir trees. Turning to look fully, he blinked in disbelief.

Damned if it wasn't that same reindeer again, with the green and red halter standing in Malcolm's field, staring right back at him.

Chapter Five

EVE SLID A steaming pancake onto Lily's plate and drizzled it with maple syrup. The chocolate chip face she'd decorated it with began to melt and slide into a frown. So she cut the pancake into bite-sized pieces.

"Does Santa like pancakes?" Lily asked, taking a bite.

"Have you seen Santa's belly?" Eve replied dryly.

Lily laughed. "My friend, Amelia, says he only likes cookies."

"Your friend is right about the cookies, but I don't think she's giving Santa enough credit for a full palate."

"What's a palate?"

"His appetite. And his sweet tooth. You know, he has a lot of homes to visit on Christmas and maybe if everyone left only cookies, he'd get bored. Fall asleep before he even finished delivering his presents. And don't forget his reindeer."

"They like pancakes, too?"

From somewhere behind her, Ben spoke. "Reindeer have very sophisticated palates. I have firsthand knowledge of that fact."

Eve reddened and turned to find him leaning on the doorjamb, having been apparently listening to their conversation. His face was flushed with cold and he shrugged out of his heavy winter jacket.

"Hi, Ben," Lily said. "Want some chocolate chip pancakes? We're 'sperimenting."

"Are we?" he said, pushing away from the door and prowling into the kitchen. "I'm a big fan of chocolate chip anything." Washing his hands, he toweled them off, watching Eve for signs of last night's argument. "If you have enough, that is."

"Of course we do," Eve said too brightly, turning to pour more batter on the griddle. "I didn't realize you were up. Where have you been?"

"Shoveling manure." Rubbing his hands together, he swung into a chair at the wooden farmhouse table cluttered at one end with bills and business paperwork that Malcolm had left.

"I thought our neighbor was going to do that."

He shrugged. "I needed the exercise."

Or he was burning off frustration with her. He looked like he hadn't slept any better than she had. She poured him a mug of coffee and added a dash of milk, the way she'd seen him do a hundred times, and handed it to him.

Wrapping his hands gratefully around the warm mug, he said, "Thanks. I can really use this."

"Rough night?" she asked with a trace of sarcasm.

"Yeah. You?"

"I slept like a baby." she lied, ruffling the little girl's hair. "We both did, right, Lily?"

"Right," Lily replied, her mouth full of pancakes. "What are we gonna do today?"

Ben shifted his gaze warily to Eve. She could guess what he was thinking. "Well, I believe the Copper Mountain Chocolate shop is first on the list. And I think Sage might have something special for us to do."

"More chocolate?" Lily clapped her hands. "And are we going to see Daddy today, too? Maybe we can bring him some chocolate 'cause he really likes it."

"You bet." Ben slugged down a few sips of coffee.

Lily twirled the feather dangling by a lace from her neck. "I think he should have this for a while. I think Mommy would like it if he did."

Eve lowered herself to her elbows on the table beside her. "Did your mom give you that feather, Lily?"

"She dropped it down for me," she said, nodding, "but he needs it more 'cause he's all by himself in the hospital."

Meeting gazes over the child's head, she and Ben exchanged looks. He shook his head quietly, indicating he'd explain about the feather later.

"Well," she told Lily, "I think it's time to get dressed so we can go on our adventure, don't you? Why don't you run upstairs and get dressed? If you need some help—"

"I don't"—the child insisted—"I can get dressed all by myself. I'm almost five years old!"

"Okay. Off you go then."

Lily polished off her last bite of pancakes and scampered upstairs, leaving the two of them alone. Eve turned Ben's pancakes on the griddle and poured herself another cup of coffee. One would not be enough after the night she'd had.

She glanced back to find him watching her. He didn't look away when she caught him. In fact, he made no move to pretend his stare was anything but what it was. Hungry.

Or maybe she was just projecting.

Should she say something about the kiss? Would he? Or should they both ignore what had happened in her doorway last night? Write it off as a bad judgment call?

"You're not going to believe what I saw out there," he said, still watching her. "I'm still not sure I believe it."

Definitely projecting. "What?"

"The reindeer. That same reindeer. Standing at the edge of Malcolm's field, staring at me."

She laughed. "That can't be."

"And yet... there he was. Halter and all."

"We're miles from the pass here. Maybe more than one escaped?"

He took a gulp of coffee. "Either way, it's a bit unnerving."

"I'll say. Stalked by Santa's minions." She bit back a grin.

"Very funny." He ran a finger across the coffee mug's

rim with a frown.

An illicit thought crossed her mind, but she distracted herself by flipping his pancakes. "Perhaps they've heard about your potential for a lump of coal this year."

A slow grin curved his mouth. "Go on. Mock. But I'll redeem myself, even if I don't like Christmas."

"We'll see." She leaned in with a wink, setting Ben's pancakes in front of him and moving the maple syrup within reach, "But remember, Rudolph will be watching."

"Can we change the subject?"

"Okay. I am going to have to check on the progress at the Graff ballroom this morning before we head to Sage's chocolate shop. Can you handle Lily alone for a little while?"

"I could," he said, without much conviction, "but why don't we come with you? There must be something we can do to help. Lily would get a kick out of seeing the place."

The idea set her back on her heels. Why couldn't Lily come? She probably would love to see the decorations. And Eve had already discovered how much Lily loved to "help."

"All right. That's a good idea, actually. Then we can stop by Sage's and see what she has for us."

Looking relieved, Ben took a bite of pancakes and rolled his eyes closed. "Mmm. And she can make pancakes, too."

THEY PRACTICALLY HAD to drag Lily out of the gorgeous Graff Hotel after spending an hour there supervising the progress of the installations and allowing her to help sprinkle "snow" on the decorated trees and islands of forest. The child had been wowed by the spectacle, not only of the ballroom, but the magical lobby, dressed to the nines in a suit of sparkle. Eve caught Ben running his fingers along the branches of a freshly cut fir and taking in the smell. With the lights up and the floor still strewn haphazardly with decorations, it wasn't possible to get the full effect. But overall, the room was beginning to take shape.

They still had the lighting to get in place and Eve had a long strategy conversation with the guy she'd hired to manage that job. Jeb Shendow, did lighting at some of the small, local theatres in Bozeman, but had worked, in years past, in Hollywood and had learned his craft well. The ballroom was going to be beautiful when they finished it.

"I'm impressed," Ben said, walking her downstairs.

"Thank you."

"I knew you did that kind of thing, but I've never seen your work up close."

"Please ignore the woman behind the curtain," she teased. "Installations are simply one-step-at-a-time magic spells. In the end, as a guest, you're not supposed to think too much about them. They're only meant to make you feel."

Even though she looked away, his eyes lingered on her. As if she, herself, were some kind magic trick he couldn't quite explain.

"I feel like chocolate," Lily put in, hopping across the carpeted lobby.

They were too early for Santa, who had a special throne in the lobby of the Graff, so they headed off to their next stop.

Outside, the town of Marietta was dressed in its Christmas best. On Main Street, storefronts were swathed in garlands and lights, and window displays, all decorated for the holiday. Snowfall this week had frosted the sidewalks and windows. All of this looked adorable in the day, but at nighttime, it took on an almost magical air. Only a week or so ago, the Christmas Stroll had taken place and Eve regretted they'd missed taking Lily to this all-town event where everyone showed up to share food and fun and stock up on Christmas gifts.

Eve glanced warily at Ben as they made their way toward Copper Mountain Chocolates, past the charmingly festooned antique store and Big Z Hardware—where an antique sleigh posed in that window, packed with tools—as well as all the rest of the shops. A half-dozen Marietta residents stopped to greet Ben warmly by name. And though he shook their hands and made nice, the shadow of Christmases past was back in his eyes again. But at least he was trying.

By the time they got to Sage's shop, Lily had slipped her hand into his and, together, they'd answered a hundred questions from her, like why people put trees indoors; who was this prince who was coming to the ball, and if Santa planned on attending, why couldn't four-year-old girls named Lily go?

The smell of chocolate wafted toward Eve the moment the little bell above the door to the shop jangled.

"Eve!" Sage Carrigan-O'Dell called from behind the counter. "What a nice surprise to see you. And Doctor Tyler?"

"Just Ben, please," he said, reaching a hand over the counter full of sweets to her.

It didn't seem to surprise him she knew who he was, since everyone seemed to. Sage was pretty and slender as a willow, despite what she did for a living, with long dark hair and an easy, welcoming smile.

"And… don't tell me this is Lily Sherman? You have grown so much since the last time I saw you," Sage said, surprised, bending down to the level of the four-year-old whose nose was pressed up against the candy case window. "It's so wonderful to see you again! Where's your daddy today?"

Eve filled her in and Sage nodded knowingly and took a deep breath. "Then I guess I know why you three are here."

"Chocolate!" Lily crowed. "And some for daddy, too."

"Before day's end, your daddy will have a nice box of chocolates sitting at his bedside. But you have to tell me what kinds he likes." She let Lily pick out a box full for Malcolm then chose one for herself. When they'd finished, Sage reached behind the counter and handed Eve an envelope she'd had waiting there. "I was hoping Malcolm would get in one of these days soon with Christmas right around the corner." She shook her head. "He's had quite a year. I'm sorry he's laid up, but I hope Patsy's plan for Lily will still be special. And you don't have to worry about the others. I'll let anyone who needs to, know what's happened. Patsy could not have been more excited to imagine her plan coming to fruition this Christmas for the two of them."

"Thanks, Sage." Eve hugged her a beat longer than necessary. "We'll make sure they both have a good one."

Eve handed the envelope to Lily. "Why don't we open it and see what's inside?"

The little girl ripped into the envelope and pulled out a handful of tickets. Ben bent down to read them. "An invitation to Carson's Christmas tree farm and eight tickets for a sleigh ride." Ben straightened. "Why eight?"

Eve was already scanning Patsy's letter, reading, "*Invite six friends to share this day with you, and treat them to a sleigh ride, because sleigh rides are always more fun with a crowd. And bring hot chocolate from Sage's shop for everyone. A thermos awaits you here.*"

Sage grinned, pulling a large thermos from a cupboard under the counter. "Yes, she even thought of that."

A sudden emotion hit Eve at the thought of Patsy working all the details out for her daughter. "Well, I think I know exactly who to call," Eve said. Bending down to Lily's ear, she whispered her idea.

Lily nodded, smiling up at Eve.

"We were just there last week buying our tree," Sage told them as she filled the thermos. "You'll have a great time. You can even pet a reindeer!"

Chapter Six

CARSON'S CHRISTMAS TREE farm was crowded with people, even this late in the season. With the holiday only a week away, Ben had assumed everyone would have already cut a tree by now, but apparently, they weren't the only ones falling behind on that task. Piped-in Christmas music played softly in the background, just loud enough to remind everyone what they were doing here.

Eve's sister, Kate and her husband, Finn, arrived with their six-year-old twins, Caylee and Cutter shortly after Eve, Lily, and Ben did. Even though the kids didn't know each other, Finn's twins welcomed Lily into their little circle with open arms and soon they'd disappeared together in the thick stand of snow-dusted pine trees for a game of hide and seek.

Ben grinned. Good to see Lily having fun. Being cooped up with two grown-ups was not her idea of a good time, he was sure of that. And while Eve was trying her best not to let the tension between the two of them interfere, it felt good to have a buffer in the form of Eve's sister and brother-in-law nearby.

"You can see there was no arm twisting required for our little hooligans to come back to the tree farm for a sleigh ride," Finn said, walking toward the freshly cut trees. "They do it up right here."

"Your kids look like they can't get enough of this place," Ben said.

"What kid wouldn't feel that way? Christmas, adventure, and candy all in one central location." Finn nodded to the teenaged girl dressed in an elf costume, standing beneath a heat lamp handing out candy canes.

In the distance, one sleigh was already returning from a run with Lane Scott, Carson's brother, at the helm of a handsome team of Percherons. Lane, a double amputee from the war, had not been Ben's patient, but he knew of him. Double amputees in a town as small as this one were known in the ortho community. But Lane had done well in his recovery, evidenced by the confident way he handled the team he was driving.

The horses blew steamy breath out into the frigid air and stamped their hooves as the sleigh came to a stop. Jingle bells on their harnesses sounded and the riders threw off the heavy blankets covering their laps which had clearly kept the passengers toasty warm.

Ben found it odd that in all the years he'd lived here in Montana, he'd never once partaken in a sleigh ride or come to a place like this. Oh, his parents had a tree—mostly for the formal parties they occasionally hosted over the holidays—a white, frosted, artificial number the help hauled out annually and finished completely decorating monochromatically by the time he'd come home from school. He could even remember a few Christmas mornings together with his parents, but mostly his memories were not of the gifts they'd put under the tree. He remembered simply wanting them to stay.

But his memories of the holidays held nothing like the fragrant scent of fresh-cut pines filling the air here or the frisson of anticipation buzzing around the children's delighted heads. He might even feel resentful at having missed this sort of delight if he hadn't so long ago let go of those sort of expectations.

Out of self-defense? Perhaps. As a kid, he'd simply occupied himself with other things at this time of year… school, sports, girls. Anything to fill the void his parents left in their wake.

Above them the cerulean blue sky was cloudless, despite last night's snow and the air felt brisk against his face. Eve's cheeks were a dusky pink with cold. She and Kate wandered off together to look at the noble firs standing near the fence line.

"So," Ben said to Finn, "do we cut our own here or buy one ready cut?"

"Your call. We cut our own this year, but if you're not into intensive manual labor, these little beauties are just as nice." He pointed to the ones lining the fence.

"I'll let Eve decide. She's the Christmas expert here."

Finn smiled. "Wise man. Must feel good to get out from behind the operating table for a little while," he said, walking toward the sleigh ride area.

"Honestly? I think I'm having withdrawals."

"I used to be the same with bull riding, though, admittedly, we're talking apples and coconuts here."

"I saw you ride last fall," Ben said. "You were incredible. But then you guys also bring me a lot of business."

Finn laughed out loud. "That's a fact. But I'm done with all that these days. Breeding bulls. That's my focus now. And as long as they don't kick me for my trouble, you and I should keep things strictly out of the hospital arena."

"Sounds fair to me."

Caylee and Cutter ran up and collided with Finn's legs, wrapping their very bundled up arms around him. Lily hung back, watching. "Can we pet the reindeer now? Lily wants to."

Sure enough, a small fenced off area complete with a small herd of reindeer sat on the other side of the sales office.

Finn hugged his twins, then swung Lily up in his arms and started toward the enclosure. "Are you an animal lover like my two, Lily?"

Charmed and surprised at once, Lily nodded shyly.

"Then I don't see much choice, do you, Ben?"

He shook his head, envying Finn's easy way with her. Lily took to Finn and the others like a baby bird who'd found her wings. He supposed this year had been especially hard on her, at four, without her mother. Without Patsy.

Ben tossed a look over at where Kate and Eve were standing under the strung up lights, pretending to look at trees, but deep in conversation. He could only imagine what Eve was bending her ear about.

"IT AIN'T OVER 'til it's over, babe," Kate said, quoting some baseball icon whose name eluded Eve.

"Well," she replied, "it—as in 'we'—never really got started so that cliché does not apply."

"He's hot for you."

"It was an apology kiss. That's all. Trust me. He didn't even mention it this morning. He probably didn't even give it a second thought. Men do not look at me and think dateable. In fact, I'm beginning to think I'm invisible to the greater dating pool."

"That's ridiculous. I know the signs. I was watching him earlier as we were arriving. The way he looked at you. Did you not notice he was standing so close he practically had his arms wrapped around you?"

"It's just crowded here," she retorted. "Anyway, I just need to get over him. I can't stay stuck on him anymore."

"My opinion? Not that you asked for it. But looking to get unstuck in the middle of a stay-cation with your main crush isn't optimal timing."

Eve shot her a look. "I sort of recall having a similar conversation with you regarding your current, and very wonderful, husband."

"Exactly. And did I listen?"

"Not exactly."

"Well, you were right. Which is why I'm telling you not to quit before the miracle."

"Miracle? Ha." Eve lifted a small, noble fir and shook the snow off the branches.

"Figure of speech. Now listen to me. He could have asked a dozen other women to do what you're doing over at Malcolm's this week. But he didn't. He asked you. Maybe because you're friends, but I think it's because—whether he planned it or not—he wedged the toe of his boot in your front door and once there, he noticed what he'd been missing."

"That's magical thinking if I ever heard it," she grumbled, wanting to change the subject. "Speaking of magical, what are you wearing to the Christmas Ball? You're going, right?"

"Assuming we can nail down a babysitter—which, so far, we have been unable to do—I bought a long, green sheath dress."

"Dad and Mom can't babysit for you?"

"Babysit? They're coming. We've got a table. They won't miss seeing a real live prince in our very midst."

"Darn." Eve said, blowing into her cold hands. A herd of

children wound through the cut trees playing tag. "I haven't made arrangements yet either. I didn't realize I'd need a babysitter when I took the job. But Ben is coming with me."

"Ahh. I have a call in to Izzy, Finn's old babysitter. If she's free, maybe she can watch all three of them. They could have a sleepover."

"That would be so awesome." She shaded her eyes with her hand, looking for the kids. "Oh, look. Ben's found the reindeer. Again."

"Eve Canaday?" The male voice came from behind her. She turned to find Chris Ackler, an old acquaintance from high school whom she hadn't seen in years, smiling down at her. She remembered him as a nerdy, chess club member whose dark hair and white-bread-with-mayonnaise looks never made him stand out. He'd gotten better looking with age, and was, nevertheless, a welcome sight in the midst of her crisis of conscience with Ben.

"Chris?"

"What a surprise," he said. "It's been a long time."

Lily chose that moment to collide with her legs in a hug. "I fed the reindeer!"

"You did?"

"She looks just like you," Chris said.

"Lily? Oh, no. She belongs to a friend. I'm just watching her for a few days."

"Ah." Two little boys ran up to him proffering reindeer-licked hands. "These two are mine. But I'm divorced. Shared custody. Just moved back here after living in Las Vegas the last few years. You look great."

"Thanks, Chris. Vegas? Wow." Was he hitting on her?

"Yeah. Didn't work out for me there. Jeez, it's so good to see you again. Yeah, so, I'm selling water filtration systems now all over Paradise Valley. You know, our water here is laden with minerals that make the water really hard."

"Really." That was a weird turn to the conversation.

"Eve," he said, "are you looking for a water filtration system for your home or business? Because I'm pretty sure I have just the right system for you." He handed her one of his business cards.

She exchanged a slow burn, '*see-what-I-mean*?' look with Kate who was biting her lips trying not to laugh.

"No, I'm not, Chris. Sorry. But if I ever do, you'll be the first one I'll call."

He nodded awkwardly. "Great. I hope so. Good to see you again."

"You, too," she said with as much sincerity as she could muster before taking Lily's hand and hurrying off to catch up with Ben.

"Hey, listen, though," she heard him calling behind her, "if you hear of anyone looking for water filtration..." She waved him a thumbs up signal without turning back.

THE ROTUND REINDEER wrangler wearing a nametag that

read "Bob" kept his eye on the children petting reindeer noses over the low fence and doled out reindeer food to small, waiting hands. Lily showed no fear, holding her palm out to a pretty doe that lapped up the food quickly from her hand. Ben had pulled out his phone and recorded the scene, knowing Malcolm would enjoy seeing it later.

When Lily finished, he washed her hands and she ran off with the twins toward Eve. He watched her collide with her in a hug. Eve was talking with some guy he didn't recognize. A guy who was very possibly hitting on her. At the very least, he was making her smile.

Ben frowned and turned back to the reindeer. He had no right to be bothered by someone asking her out. In fact, he was sure it happened all the time. But bother crept up his throat all the same and lodged somewhere between reason and want.

It had not escaped his notice that these reindeer also wore glittery, colored halters, similar to the one on his close, personal nemesis. "Have you lost a reindeer lately?" he asked Bob, the reindeer wrangler.

This earned him a puzzled look. "Nope. I keep track of all my girls. Why?"

"I've spotted one twice now, running loose," Ben said, "wearing a halter similar to those. It's clearly not wild."

"Probably an elk," the old man said, "or a trick of light."

A trick of light? He didn't think so. "Anyone else keep penned reindeer around here?"

"Santa," Bob replied with a wink.

Ben snorted quietly. He'd probably never catch sight of that animal again, nor was it his problem to see it got back to its rightful owner. There was plenty of food around to keep it alive.

"Sleigh ride anyone?"

From somewhere behind him, he heard Eve's voice. He turned to find her holding Lily's hand. Kate and Finn were pulling up the rear, wrangling the twins.

Eve's eyes were bright but her smile was wary. "I think they've exhausted the hide and seek possibilities."

For a moment, he felt tongue-tied watching her. He imagined—just for a heartbeat—her standing beside him, holding their own child's hand… a mother, as he supposed she was meant to be, looking at him the way Kate did her husband, Finn.

Illogical, he thought, in his best Spock voice. Not for him. He wouldn't have a clue how to parent a child and he'd probably bungle the whole thing. He was heading to Honduras and she was meant for a man who could give her those things she wanted. Like maybe that guy who'd just been making eyes at her.

Still, he reached for Lily's free hand and she readily gave it and closed her small fingers around his. "What do you say, Lily? Ever been on a sleigh ride?"

Lily shook her head. If she had, she would be too young to remember doing it with her mom. "So this'll be a first.

For you and for me."

Eve poured a cup of hot chocolate for everyone as they waited in line. Ben and Finn discussed Malcolm's pregnant mare while Kate and Eve chatted with the kids. When it was their turn, they loaded onto the sleigh Lane Scott was driving. He and Finn joked about being long lost brothers from another father with the same last name.

The horses lurched forward and began trotting down the trail.

"Having fun?" he asked Eve, who had settled beside him beneath the pile of blankets.

"I am. I love this tradition. I think I haven't ever missed a year. Then, we're lucky up here, with all this snow. But I guess you won't miss all this in the jungles of Honduras. All that green."

He glanced around at the sparkling white landscape. All that green had enticed him and not for a moment had he imagined he'd miss the cold, long winters of Montana. But he supposed that was because they'd always felt lonely to him. Long and lonely. With family around, friends, he guessed winter here had its charms. He was sitting in one of them right now beside the one person who had made winter here more bearable.

"I will miss it," he said. "More than I thought I would."

Her gaze slid away and she sipped the last of her hot chocolate.

They followed the trodden trail around the forest of

Christmas trees, down a wide path thick with firs and ancient ponderosa pines that towered above them. Giant pinecones dangled from the branches like ornaments and littered the snow along the path. The landscape was postcard pretty and widened ahead into a view of the whole valley.

"What lake is that?" Finn asked, pointing to a smallish lake in the distance.

"That's Miracle Lake," Lane said from the driver's seat. "You all know the legend about that place, right?"

Ben didn't.

"A legend?" Cutter asked, wide-eyed, wanting to know.

"Well, the story goes that place is special. Maybe has some kind of special powers. A few things have happened there to give it that name. Seems years ago, nobody really remembers now when it was, a child nearly drowned there in the winter. Fell under the ice and it took a while to find him. But when they did, he revived like a miracle and went on to live a long life."

Ben smiled to himself. Not so much miracle as the human capacity to hibernate. Slow the heartbeat to nearly a stop in icy water. But most did attribute such things to miracles. And back in the day, such a scenario was improbable if not considered impossible.

"And then," Lane continued, "there was the woman whose cancer disappeared after she went into those waters one summer. There have been other things, enough to garner a whole mystical reputation. But a lot of folks believe the waters have some magical powers. Hence the name. Miracle Lake. But you know, it's just a legend."

"What's a legend?" Lily asked.

"A story that gets told over and over until maybe what wasn't quite real about it seems true," Eve told her. "Or maybe it was true all the time."

Ben glanced down at Lily who was raptly listening, holding her feather. He wondered if she was thinking about Patsy and if Miracle Lake could have saved her, too? Lily brushed the white vane of feathers against her lips.

Beside him, Eve was probably thinking the same thing, because she started an 'I-spy' game with the children to distract them. The rest of the ride the children spent looking for wildlife, after spotting a deer standing in the meadow.

The horses' bells jangled the whole way and Ben couldn't help but imagine when this country was traversed exactly this way, without cars or cell phones interfering in the spectacular beauty that was this valley. With the snowcapped Absarokas in the distance and Copper Mountain looming over Marietta—stunning at sunset with its copper-colored hues—he remembered what had called him back to this place after many years away.

Yet, except for his daily runs—head down and mentally reviewing his upcoming surgeries—he'd sequestered himself in the hospital or his home instead of enjoying this place. Two and a half years had flown by in a rush of work and more work. The nurses were right to bet against him taking a vacation. He would still be working right now if it wasn't for Lily. And Eve.

Pressed warmly against his side, Eve flicked a look his way. For a long moment, she stared at him, as if trying to puzzle him out, then she smiled and looked away.

Ben got out his phone and recorded the last of the ride, and Lily's laughter at Cutter's wolf howl. The three of them started howling then and when they were done, Ben texted the video to Malcolm, saying "*Wanted you along for the ride. Lily's having fun.*"

After the sleigh ride, the seven of them trudged into the Christmas tree farm and found a perfect little tree to cut and take home. The group decision took the pressure off of Ben. He was happy to let the others choose. After they paid, Carson Scott handed Ben the next envelope. Inside, Patsy's letter to Malcolm with instructions on how to decorate the tree tonight and where to find the ornaments.

When it was time to head home, they tied the Noble fir on top of Ben's car, said goodbye to the Scotts and promised another play date soon.

LILY FELL ASLEEP as soon as they hit the road and Eve turned some satellite Christmas music on low. The day had been full of laughter and exercise, and contentment ebbed through her. She loved spending time outdoors in the winter, when the air was crisp and scented with pines and the snow cushioned the landscape with white. "That wasn't so bad, now was it?" she asked Ben.

"No, not bad at all," he admitted. "In fact, virtually painless."

A smile tugged at her mouth. "That's the best you can say?"

He chuckled. "Okay. I liked it. I had fun. I haven't had a day like that in a long time."

On the radio, John Legend sang "This Christmas" and she idly wondered if JL had been spying on her life. The day had gone better than she'd imagined it would after last night, but still, she felt unresolved around Ben. As if she were waiting for some invisible other shoe to drop.

Ben broke into her thoughts. "So… uh, who was that guy you were talking to?"

She frowned. "Guy?"

"Yeah, over by the tree lot. Before the sleigh ride."

Sliding her mind back, she landed on the water filtration mogul. "You mean Chris Ackler?" She narrowed a look at him. "Why?"

"No reason." He shrugged, but flicked a look at her. "He looked familiar."

"He was a few years behind you in school. I doubt you knew him." She settled deeper into the leather seat of his Lexus and stared at the lines on the highway.

"He looked, I don't know… interested in you."

"Maybe he was asking me out." A lie, but he *did* ask her

to call him. About… water filtration.

"You said yes?"

She slid a look his way. Was he… jealous? "Really, Ben, I don't see how that would matter to you."

"You haven't even mentioned our kiss last night."

Surprise made her catch her breath. "Well, neither have you… after the apology, I mean."

"It wasn't—" He started again. "I wasn't apologizing for the kiss. I was apologizing for not telling you the truth."

"Then why'd you kiss me?"

A muscle worked in his jaw.

"It's a simple answer, Ben—i.e., I had a little too much wine… I was overtired… I wasn't thinking straight…"

"I wanted to," he explained, glancing in the rear-view mirror at Lily, who was still sleeping. "You liked it, didn't you? At least, it felt like you did."

"Of course I liked it. Obviously, I liked it. Who doesn't like kissing?"

"What about kissing *me*?"

Is it warm in here? I think it's warm in here. With a shake of her head, she rolled the window down halfway. The frigid air tugged at her hair and she leaned toward the opening, breathing deeply.

"Of course, kissing you," she answered softly. "Unless… unless it's because I'm convenient?"

"*What*? No. Eve. *God.* How could you even think that?"

"Because"—she warned—"I am not convenient. Not at

all. I'm relatively inconvenient if you want to know the truth. And I have no interest in being another notch in your bedpost."

If he was insulted, he simply laughed. "Well, that's good, because I only notch my stick shift."

She jerked a look down at it before feeling the burn of embarrassment. He didn't even *have* a stick shift.

"Geez, Eve."

"You are aware you have a reputation, Doctor *Mc*Tyler," she teased.

"Don't you call me that, too. Look, I can count on one hand the women—"

She stuck her fingers in her ears and sang along with the radio. "*Jingle bells, jingle bells, jingle all the—*"

"Okay. Fine. Fine. Those few women in my past have nothing to do with you. Or maybe they do. Maybe they're exactly why I haven't"—he checked the backseat in the mirror again—"why I've stayed away from you… that way."

That way?

She folded her arms. "So you're saying you would have kissed me sometime in the last… oh, say year, but for your reputation?"

"I'm saying I would have kissed you before if we weren't such good friends. I didn't want to screw that up. I still don't. Those other…" He squinted at the fading light as the sun set over the mountains. "Those others were just… they weren't important to me."

She flattened a disbelieving palm across her chest. “And I am?”

“Of coursc you are. I care about you.”

People cared about their lawns. Or even their golden retrievers. No, “*I care about you*” was not the phrasing she was looking for. Not even close.

“Well,” she said, staring out the window, “that’s just a moot point now, isn’t it? You’re leaving for the big world and I’m just a small-town girl staying here in Marietta. So, let’s just agree to keep things the way they were, okay? Friends. No more kissing… etcetera.” If Kate could only hear her now.

“Right. Okay. Friends,” he said, more quickly than she would have liked. Or at all, honestly.

She sank back in her seat, feeling worse than she had before their little talk and a long silence stretched between them. Miles rolled by as the sun winked out behind the mountains and soon darkness revealed a wash of stars in the inky sky overhead. There was nothing like the Montana night sky in winter. So sharp and crystal clear. Full of possibility and wonder. But tonight those stars made Eve feel small and wildly out of control of the destiny she’d imagined for herself—which, admittedly, was a contradiction of terms. Destiny had its own agenda and rarely agreed with her.

She would take the blame herself for allowing time to slip away between her and Ben. For not being more assertive with her own wants and desires. For letting him believe friendship was enough for her and for accepting that, as well. But starting something up now seemed foolish and doomed to fail.

And yet… wasn't that the same kind of thinking that had gotten her into this mess?

What had Olivia said? "*If you're unhappy with how it's going, change it.*"

But how?

Chapter Seven

THEY STOPPED AT the hospital on the way home because Lily needed to see Malcolm and he needed to see her. Ben carried her in after Eve woke her and they found Malcolm awake with Nurse Kelly Reynolds lingering by his bedside. The two of them were laughing about something while eating Sage's chocolates as he, Lily and Eve walked in.

Ben took in the pair and smiled. "You're looking better today."

Kelly blushed and jumped up. "He's doing well, Doctor Tyler. Healing up nicely. We were just—"

"Talking," Malcolm finished for her. "Kelly was just telling me about the time two Christmases ago when you dressed up as the jolly, old man himself for the children's floor."

Eve swiveled a disbelieving look at him.

Ben shrugged. "What? I was boonswaggled into it. No one else fit the costume. And everyone else was home with their families."

"What jolly old man?" Lily asked, her look swinging between the adults.

"Oh," Eve answered quickly. "Just a gentleman who visits this hospital every year to spread a little cheer."

"Oh." She laughed. "I thought you meant Santa."

"On that note," Kelly said, flicking a smile at Malcolm, "I'm going to get back to work." And with that, she gracefully excused herself from the room.

Malcolm reached his arms out to Lily. "How's my girl?"

Ben lowered her down to him for a kiss, but didn't allow full contact. "We have to still be careful of his stitches," he said.

Lily launched into a full description of the day they'd had and Malcolm listened raptly. At the intricacy of Patsy's plans for him, he could only smile. Ben handed him the latest letter, which included a personal message for Malcolm, though he had accidentally read it.

Moved again by the sweetness of Patsy's love for Mal, Ben could only imagine what such devotion might feel like on the receiving end. He was clearly no good at such things, as evidenced by Eve's reaction to their kiss. But she was right about one thing. He needed to stay the hell away from her this week and not make matters worse by hurting her more.

"I feel like such a jerk, lying here in bed when Patsy went to all this trouble for me and Lily."

"All these letters," Eve said, "we will save for you for next year. This Christmas, you'll have to get by with a little help from your friends."

Gratefully, Malcolm accepted that. "How's the mare? Any sign of labor yet?"

Ben lifted Malcolm's chart, automatically scanning it. "I'll check her tonight. She was fine this morning. We're keeping her in the barn until she delivers. No good having a brand new foal out in this kind of cold."

"Good call."

Lily lifted the feather necklace off and handed it to Malcolm. "This is for you, Daddy."

"What? Your feather? No. You should keep it."

"No, Mommy says you should keep it because you're all by yourself in here."

Malcolm slid a look between Eve and Ben.

"Mommy said that, did she?"

"Uh-huh. Last night in my room. But you keep it just for a little while. And then I'll get it back."

"Thank you, darlin'," he said, kissing her cheek. "I could use one of mommy's angel feathers in here."

Frankly, Ben didn't think perpetuating such mythology with children was healthy. The feather clearly belonged to a swan or a snow goose or some other passing bird. And he suspected Lily had become overly attached to the thing, since she wouldn't be without it, except to help her father. Already she'd invented a conversation with Patsy about Malcolm. But it wasn't his place to say what fantasies people should cling to. Least of all a four-year-old girl. After all, weren't they about to tell a big fat lie to her about the jolly, old man himself?

They only stayed a little longer before saying good night and driving home to the ranch. While Eve made them dinner, Ben set up the tree, then went out to check on the mare. Jonas had already swung by to put the other horses up for the night, and everyone was fed and bedded down already. Jonas had left him a note, saying that she was showing signs. But that could mean anything from twenty-four hours to three or four more days before she actually delivered her foal. He would be checking on her first thing in the morning.

Ben patted her velvety nose. "Getting ready, are you, girl? Hang in there. I'll make sure Jonas takes good care of you and your baby."

The mare answered with a soft nicker, pressing her forehead to the palm of his hand.

He closed the barn up for the night and went back inside. Eve had located the ornaments in the basement and had half the tree decorated with Lily by the time he arrived. She was standing beside the tree, reaching up to hang an ornament, as he walked in. The smell of something delicious wafted from the kitchen.

Caught in an unwary moment, she smiled over at him—the headlamp smile of hers that lit up a room.

Good Lord.

When had she begun to have this unnerving effect on him? When exactly had a simple smile from her been sufficient to get him hard, or cause him to imagine her mouth pressed up against his until she panted for breath?

What the hell was wrong with him, starting up conversations about kisses he couldn't—and had no right to—finish? He'd thought about their discussion in the car earlier, dammit, and had decided she was right. He'd known it all along, really. There was absolutely no point in burrowing any deeper into feelings for each other at this impasse. No point at all.

Apparently not thinking along those same lines at all, she chirped, "Look what I found in the ornament box." Waving a piece of paper at him, she seemed apparently oblivious to his discomfort, while he occupied himself hanging up his jacket, turning deliberately away from her until he felt decent enough to turn back. When that didn't happen, he said, "Be right there. I'm going to get a beer." With that, he disappeared into the kitchen and stood, staring vacantly before the open refrigerator door, willing his erection away.

Women. He would never grasp their complexities or gracefully manage their effect on him. While his monkey brain chattered on, goading him about the kiss they'd shared last night, his rational brain coached him in the rules he'd always played by. The ones that kept him a safe distance from exactly this kind of mess.

The rules that had him on his way to the sweltering jungles of Honduras.

"*If you've decided the best thing for you to do with your life is run off to the jungles of Honduras, instead of staying in Marietta and facing whatever it is that's scaring you away, a place where people actually need and care about you, then who am I to try and stop you?*"

He wasn't scared, dammit. He was just… oh, hell…

"You all right?" Eve asked, suddenly beside him.

He practically jumped, but reached for a beer. "Fine."

"You've been standing there awhile."

"Have I? I guess I'm just tired."

"I found another letter," she said. "In the box of ornaments. Patsy really thought of everything."

A smile tugged at his mouth. That was Patsy. "What's next?"

"A visit with Santa Claus, of course. And a recipe for reindeer food. Maybe you can make that happen tomorrow while I'm at the Graff."

He swallowed thickly. Tomorrow night was the ball. He might be on his own for the day and the thought terrified him.

"But that's not all," Eve continued, proffering the letter. "You can read it."

"*I want her to learn that Christmas is as much about giving as receiving. So please, let her help you make the reindeer food (all the ingredients are listed below) and take it to the children's floor at the hospital and let her help you distribute the goodie bags for all the kids stuck there for Christmas. Just in case Rudolph needs extra incentive to find them there.*"

He could probably manage that little craft project alone

and at least it would put him back on his home turf for part of the day. And, bonus, Lily could see Malcolm.

"We forgot the angel on top," Lily yelled from the other room. "I'll put her on."

Ben and Eve hurried back in to find that Lily had pulled a chair near the tree and was doing her best impression of her father's risky practices. Swooping her safely into his arms, Ben made her giggle as he lifted her high enough to place the white-robed angel at the top of the tree, where she glinted in the colored tree lights, all shimmery with tiny seed pearls and sequins.

With her skinny arms back around Ben's neck, Lily said, "Look, Ben. She looks just like mommy."

And outside, Ben could have sworn he heard the jingle of bells.

Chapter Eight

THE NEXT AFTERNOON Ben stood with Lily in line for Santa at the Graff, behind a handful of children and their parents. Already they'd waited a half hour for the jolly old man and Lily was dancing in front of him, spinning from his hand. They'd already spent the morning at the hospital, handing out reindeer food and he suddenly realized his error in not making a tactical stop sooner when she announced, "I have to go potty."

Oh, no. "You do?" He scanned the lobby for rest rooms, wondering how he was going to manage this little delicacy.

"Uh-huh. Really, really bad."

Ben leaned in to the woman in front of him. "Could you save our spot. She's gotta—"

"Sure, no worries."

He could run her up to Eve, who he guessed was still upstairs in the ballroom, but he didn't want to bother her. It was a matter of honor that he'd managed this day all on his own with Lily so far. He wasn't about to drop the proverbial ball now.

He found the restrooms, but that helped his dilemma not at all. Should he take her in the men's room? Let her go alone into the ladies? A mother with a small daughter happened upon them just then and stopped to help.

"You want me to take her in with us? I'll watch her. Don't worry."

Relief swamped him. "Would you? I'm not sure what the right thing is here."

"C'mon," she told Lily, "you can come with Jessica and me."

"I'll wait for you right here, Lily," he said as the two little girls went inside, sizing each other up with shy glances.

Was that the right thing? He worried for the next five minutes, standing outside the ladies' room. Should he have taken her himself? How the heck did real fathers figure these things out?

No sooner had he decided that he'd handled it all wrong then Lily skipped out of the bathroom with Jessica holding hands. "Can Jessica see Santa with me? We can go together."

Gratefully, he smiled up at the mom. "You can have our place in line if you want. Thank you so much."

"Don't worry about it for a second. We're not in any hurry. I wish all dads were as loving as you to their little girls."

Her words practically knocked the wind out of him. "She's not—" he began, but he decided not to make a big deal of it and Lily was too preoccupied to notice. "She can't quite manage all on her own yet. Thank you."

"Have fun visiting with Santa," the woman told Lily. And they headed off to the end of the Santa line.

The woman who'd held their place was virtually next up and she motioned them over. "Your turn," she said, smiling down at Lily, whose eyes had gone wide at the sight of Santa waiting for her.

She settled onto the red-suited man's lap without a moment's hesitation.

"I hear your name is Lily," he said gruffly, smiling down at her.

She sent a shocked look up at Ben. How had he known that? Ben just smiled.

Lily nodded wordlessly.

"So tell me what's on your list for Christmas, Lily? What do you want to ask me for?"

"My daddy got a boo-boo. I just want him to come home for Christmas."

"A boo-boo?" Santa glanced up at Ben questioningly, like he'd assumed he was her father. "Well, now, that's too bad. What's your daddy's name, Lily? So I can write it down on my own list. To remember, you know."

"*Daddy*," she answered in all seriousness.

"It's Malcolm," Ben supplied. "Malcolm Sherman."

"Ah, I see," Santa replied sagely. He licked the tip of his short little pencil and scribbled down Malcolm's name in his book. "There. I'll see what I can do about your daddy. But those kinds of requests are a little trickier. Is there anything else you want? A dolly maybe? A book?"

Lily shook her head, then reconsidered. "Maybe a puppy."

"Ho-ho-ho!" the whiskered one laughed. "All right then. You do like to make Santa's job a challenge." He pulled a small candy cane from a bag near his knee. "This is for you, angel." He pulled an envelope from behind him somewhere and handed it to Ben. "And this, apparently, is for you, Doctor Tyler."

"*He knows everything*," Lily whispered to Ben, wide-eyed.

Ben took the envelope and helped Lily hop down. "Thanks, Santa," he said.

"Do you promise about my dad?" Lily asked the whiskered old man.

"I promise I'll do my best, Lily."

An elf came to usher them out of Santa's workshop and Ben walked her to the luxurious couches nearby and, without warning, Lily climbed onto his lap. He swallowed hard.

"How'd you like that?" he asked her as she opened the cellophane on her candy cane.

She nodded. "Do you think he'll keep his promise?"

"He's Santa, isn't he?"

"What did he give you that for?" she asked pointing to the envelope in his hand. "What does it say?"

"Well…" He slid a finger under the envelope flap and opened it. "Let's see." He intended to improvise. Say something about books being great Christmas presents. But when he opened the letter, he saw Patsy's handwriting again. There was the usual, the final instruction to take Lily caroling. And a final line at the end, written to Malcolm alone as the last task.

It read, "*Find someone to love.*"

Ben's heart thudded and stuttered, and for reasons he couldn't fathom, he looked up at the balcony that bordered the next floor. Standing at the rail, watching him and Lily, stood Eve with a strange, unreadable look on her face. How long had she been standing there? When caught looking, she finger-waved at him with a bittersweet smile, then turned back to the ballroom and disappeared.

And he felt… bereft.

"What does it say?" Lily repeated, tugging at the letter her mother had written to her father.

Ben pulled his gaze back to the letter. He gave her a little hug. "It says, 'Merry Christmas'."

THAT EVENING, AT precisely seven-fifty, Eve heard the doorbell ring. Of all the times for Ben to be prompt, much less early, it had to be now. She been running around like a chicken with its tail feathers on fire all day and had not caught up.

Panicked, she spilled the contents of her makeup bag across the counter and chased her lipstick into the sink. With a feeling of doom pounding behind her eyes, she stared at her half-ready self in the mirror with a frown. Her makeup couldn't quite hide the still-healing air bag abrasion on her cheek and the curls in her hair hadn't turned out exactly the way she'd wanted.

Settle down. It's only a ball.

A ball with Ben.

But her ridiculously low-cut, sleeveless, crimson gown was only half-zipped up the back and she couldn't seem to locate her other shoe. She tugged at the bodice of her dress, trying to rearrange it. No use. Oh, why hadn't she'd bought a backup?

She reached for the zipper, but still couldn't grasp it. "Be right there!" she called and kicked off the shoe on her right foot. She'd deal with that later.

At the front door, she undid the deadbolt and swung open the door. "You're early! You won't believe this but I've lost a—" she began, but saw that it wasn't Ben at all, but a woman standing on her doorstep. "Oh. Hello. I… I was expecting someone else. Can I help you?"

Dark-haired, with soulful blue-green eyes that reminded her of someone she couldn't place, the woman was stamping her feet in the cold and rubbing her gloved hands together before taking in the ball gown Eve was wearing.

"Oh. I'm sorry," the woman said. "This is a bad time."

"I—" Eve broke off, confused. "If you're selling something, it really is a bad time."

The woman blinked up at her, looking lost. Her grey coat was simple and probably more than a few seasons old if the frayed cuffs were any indication. Eve glanced behind her to the sidewalk near the street where some kind of a suitcase stood waiting.

"Wait. You're not selling water filters, are you?"

"Water filters? No."

Eve sighed, strangely relieved. "Okay. Well, whatever it is, I'm sorry. I'm really not interested. Have a nice night." She made to close the door, but the woman spoke again.

"I'm not selling anything… except myself, actually." She proffered a manila envelope from under her arm with a quick smile. "You're Eve. Canaday, right? I'm answering the ad you placed in the Marietta Courier last week for a wedding photographer. That's my resume there and a sample of my work."

Eve blinked at her, confused. "Oh. I… usually don't meet applicants at my home. How did you—?"

"I shouldn't have, I know. But face-to-face always beats a cold resume. And… since I just got into town tonight, I thought I'd drop mine off in person. You weren't that hard to find, actually."

That's disconcerting. There was something about this woman. Something weirdly familiar, yet Eve couldn't remember having met her before. She looked a few years older than her. Maybe Kate's age.

She read the name on the resume envelope aloud. "Alessandra Thibeaux?"

"Ali." the woman corrected. "Listen, I can see you're getting ready to go out. That's a great dress, by the way. I'm sorry to have bothered you. But I really would love the job." She hesitated. "I *need* the job. But if I've already offended you by coming here, I apologize."

"Wait," Eve called as the woman headed down the snowy steps. Something niggled at Eve, but she couldn't put her finger on what, besides being discomforted by how easy it had been for a stranger to locate her home. "Do I… know you from somewhere?"

Ali tipped a look up at Eve through her eyelashes. "No. No, we've definitely never met. I'd remember."

Eve nodded. She wouldn't hire her. She knew nothing about Alessandra Thibeaux, except that she had no idea about job hiring protocol. Or personal space. "Okay. I'll take a look at your shots and I'll call you if I'm interested. Sound fair?"

"Thank you. Really. And I'm sorry for the timing. Good night." Head up, Ali made her way down the sidewalk to the street just as Ben stepped out of his Lexus at the end of her sidewalk.

Eve nearly gasped at the sight of him, looking movie-star handsome in his tux, heading her way. He nodded a hello to Ali as he passed her, then turned a curious expression on Eve.

Then he stopped dead on the sidewalk, and with George Clooney drama, threw his arms out wide. "Oh, my God.

Look at you."

Self-conscious and freezing in the open doorway, Eve laughed, clamped her arms across her nearly bare bosom and motioned him in. "And dare I say Hollywood has nothing on you. You, sir, should wear a tux every day." She shut the door behind him, rubbing her bare arms.

Her words pleased him, she could tell, but he'd been undressing her with his eyes since he got out of his car. "You look amazing, Eve."

Oh, dear. "Thank you." Nervous, she brushed her hair off her shoulder. "But I can't zip my zipper. Could you, um…?"

She turned around and he did the honors. "Who was that, leaving?" he asked.

"Just someone looking for a job. Going about it all wrong." But then, who was she to judge? Look at her record with Ben.

He made a sound in his throat. "There you go."

When she turned back, he was standing too close. For a moment, she thought he meant to kiss her again. In fact, she was almost sure he would, but he took a reluctant step back instead.

"That dress is—"

"Low-cut. I know. I don't know what I was thinking."

"I was going to say—spectacular. Whatever you were thinking," he said, his gaze panning down her like a caress, "I concur."

She'd bought this gown before any of this had happened with him. When she was sure he'd be thousands of miles away from here and if she had to suffer through attending the ball alone, the very least she could do was try to make herself feel pretty. Now, she just felt exposed.

She swallowed hard and reached for the gorgeous three-inch heeled Christian Louboutin she'd kicked off at the door. "You're very kind. And a bit early. So can you help me find my other shoe?"

"Tell me where to look."

They searched her small apartment, living room, den and finally, her bedroom. Too late—in fact, the moment he bent to look under the dust ruffle on her bed, she realized she'd left her vibrator plugged in there. The instant she remembered, she gasped audibly.

And the instant *he* saw it, he straightened, flicking a look at her that evolved into a sexy grin. "I, uh, didn't see your shoe."

Hands on her hips, she said, "So I have a vibrator under my bed. Wanna make somethin' of it?"

He church-steepled his fingers over his lips, trying to keep a straight face. "Now there's a loaded question."

"Ugh. You weren't supposed to see that. I just forgot it was there. Anyway, I—I use it for sore muscles." *And men read Playboy for the articles.* She reached a hand up to her shoulder and massaged it dramatically. "This, for instance, is from that light swag that wouldn't stay hung. And right here"—she bracketed her neck with her hands—"the 'snow' that refused to stay where I put it." Actually, now that she thought of it, she *was* sore from working all day hanging decorations.

With a chuckle, Ben stood and walked toward her. "Yeah?" He reached out and replaced her hand with his. "Here?"

"No, you don't have to—*ohhh.*" *Mercy…*

"Right here?"

"Uh-huh."

"And here?" His big hands seemed to know where every knot was and found them with unerring precision. Like the surgeon he was.

"*Ohhhh, yes.* That feels…"

"Good?"

She sighed. "Yes."

He moved his hands to her neck, sliding his fingers into her hair at the base of her skull, taking surprising care not to mess her hair up. She tipped her head forward, allowing him better access. Her embarrassment over her little secret under her bed shifted into want.

Nothing could stop the thrill that chased up her spine at the feel of his hands on her. Or deny ache inspired by the warm brush of his breath on her neck when he leaned close. Why was he touching her like this? Why, unless he meant to do the one thing they'd both decided they couldn't—*shouldn't*—do.

His thumbs massaged her neck in long, languid strokes. What was the point of trying to deny her feelings for him? Would it really keep her heart any safer when he left, to deny herself the happiness of now? Would it matter one way or another if they made love instead of staying platonic? As consenting adults with a clear vision of the inevitable?

He slid his hands down her neck and bracketed her shoulders from behind, staying any intentions she might have had to ask for a kiss. For a long moment, he didn't speak. Didn't say anything. As if he were trying to find some point of balance he'd lost. Then he pressed his mouth against the side of her throat in a kiss that reached all the way to her toes.

"I promised I wouldn't do this," he said against her skin, sliding his mouth up the length of her neck.

He nibbled on her earlobe and Eve felt her knees go weak.

"You did. You absolutely did." She let her head fall back against his shoulder. Heat smoldered through her.

"With good reason," he added, dipping his tongue into the edge of her ear.

"What reason was that again?"

His arms curled around her waist. "I can't remember."

"Oh, wait. Wait. It's coming to me. We're trying to get out, unscathed."

"Impossible," he said, "and, I'm thinking… highly overrated."

"Is it?" She rested her hands on his strong forearms. "Why, again, is that?"

He turned her in his arms. "Because no one gets out unscathed. No one."

Dropping his mouth onto hers, his kiss this time was almost nothing like the last one. This kiss was not apologetic or even tentative, but, instead, full of all of the angst and craziness of the last few days. All of the moments, he'd looked in her eyes and admitted there was more to them than simple friendship.

His tongue plundered her mouth and she welcomed him in. She tasted the sweetness of his breath and the snow-fresh air from outside on him. But all she could think was, *finally*. Threading her fingers into his hair, she pulled him closer still and any space left between them vanished. No mistaking his desire for her as it pressed up against her. Rock hard with want. Dampness gathered between her legs.

No one gets out unscathed. True enough. For she could already feel her heart breaking with the hunger of his kiss.

He backed her up against the bed and together they dropped down against the mattress, her atop him. Her breasts pressed up against his chest and in this dress, she imagined she was practically indecent.

Breaking the kiss, she swallowed thickly before lifting her head to look down at him. "So," she asked, with a small grin, "what are you saying?"

"I'm trying not to talk," he said, still breathing hard from the kiss. "Talking just screws everything up. I'm better with my hands."

She nodded. "Surgeon. A man of action."

"Uh-huh."

"I'm wrinkling your tux."

"There's an easy fix for that."

She knew he was about to say, "take it off". But before the words could leave his mouth, her cell phone rang on the bedside table. Eve glared up at it. *Do not answer it. Do not—*

He slid a look in that direction, too. "You need to get that?"

Did she? Only the biggest event in town was happening as they spoke and she had a small, miniscule part in it—that merely her entire reputation was staked on…

It rang again. "Um, I might need to check…" Reluctantly, she crawled off him and reached for the hated thing. Sure enough, the caller ID said Sarah. Her primary assistant at the ball. *Oh, no.*

"Hello?"

"Eve!" Sarah's voice sounded semi-hysterical. In the background, the sound of the crowd was a deep hum. "The sugar plum fairy is in pieces on the floor!"

"*What*? Oh no!" Her centerpiece ice sculpture, one of three a local artist had carved for this event.

"Oh, yes. No one is copping to how it happened, but I've already got a crew cleaning her up. I already called to see if we could replace her, but Hans has got nothing. The doors open in ten minutes. We need you here. ASAP!"

"On my way now," she said and hung up. She must have done something wrong, somewhere to deserve this terrible timing. "I have to go. I'm sorry. Crisis. Nothing that can't be fixed, but they need me."

Ben shoved himself upright and straightened out his hair with one hand. "Then we'll go. Now."

"I'm really sorry." He'd never know how sorry.

"Don't be. It's your job. It's important. This can wait."

"Can it?" Those old demons were back, just as quickly as they'd disappeared, telling her that moment of abandon had been her imagination and when she looked back it would all go *Poof*!

He grabbed her hand. "Eve. This thing between you and me, it's complicated. But it seems foolish to deny that something's there when"—he gestured to the bed—"*that* happens. We'll figure it out. But now, we'll go."

Her family would be there. All of them. Waiting to see if she'd taken a stand with him or not. But to jeopardize this fragile new leaf between them seemed—no, *felt*—dangerous. She suddenly wished she could just bow out on the ball and finish what they'd just begun. But that would be too easy. No, she'd just have to suck it up and get through tonight. And, after all, it wasn't every night a girl got to go to a ball with her fantasy boyfriend. Or her best friend.

Chapter Nine

IT STARTED TO snow as they reached the Graff. Big, fat, juicy flakes drifting past the streetlamps at the entrance to the gala framed the night in what Ben could only describe as magic. The whole place was like a picture off a Christmas card, but the centerpiece was Eve in that red dress, her shoulders covered in a gorgeous faux fur wrap, looking as delicious as he'd ever seen her.

He helped her out of the car, popped up an umbrella he kept there for emergencies such as this and pulled her toward him. "Did I mention how beautiful you look tonight?" he murmured close to her ear.

"Stop. You're making me blush."

She tucked a strand of dark hair behind one ear, but the smile on her face told him his words pleased her. He wanted to please her. He wanted to make this night special for her.

"That's the idea," he parried with a grin. "You ready to go in?"

She took a deep breath and nodded. They started to walk but she threaded her fingers through his and stopped him.

"Thanks, Ben. For coming with me. I'm actually a little nervous tonight."

"Absolutely my pleasure." He kissed her, a quick, heated press of his mouth on hers because he couldn't resist her when she looked at him that way.

And because he'd thought of little else since they'd kissed earlier. It was going to be hard to keep his hands off her tonight. He wasn't sure what was happening between them but it was hitting him like a sucker punch to the gut. "Don't be nervous. The place looks amazing. And so do you."

She tucked her arm into his and gave him a little hug as they made their way inside. And for a moment, Ben felt outside himself, watching her do it. Like a déjà vu moment when some kind of clarity strikes, or reminds someone of what they should already know. She felt right in his arms. And he felt something close to happy for the first time in a long time.

While Eve contended with her crisis, Ben checked in at the check in table at the entrance, then shouldered his way through the crowded dance floor alone on his way to his assigned table—the Canaday table. Walking into the ballroom of the Graff was like walking into a winter wonderland. He had to give it to her, she had outdone herself with this place. In three corners, giant Christmas trees, all beribboned and sparkling with lights and ornaments, and dusted with artificial snow, stood mingling with white painted bare trees sparkling with white lights. Smaller fir trees mingled beneath them. A winding, wooden walkway threaded around the perimeter between the mini-forests.

The lighting, dimmed to reflect the beautiful trees, highlighted the centerpiece tables where shimmering ice sculptures glistened, surrounded by ribbon-wrapped garlands. Overhead, hundreds of Mylar balloons bobbed against the ceiling, dangling shiny silver and gold strings and a sweeping light made them look like fireworks overhead.

At every doorway, mistletoe balls hung, but giant balls of the stuff also dangled randomly from the ceiling in spots likely to inspire kisses. He thought of Patsy and how she would have loved being here and, in the same moment, realized how alike she and Eve really were.

She'd dragged him—kicking—into Christmas this year and he had to admit, it hadn't been as bad as he'd feared. In fact, he'd had fun. From the sleigh ride to the tree farm to taking Lily today to see Santa. Even making reindeer food wasn't the chore he'd imagined, but a small dose of optimism in a cynical world, seen through Lily's eyes and those of the children with whom she'd shared the gifts of reindeer food in the hospital.

Now, here he was at a Christmas ball. If not for her, he'd be sequestered in some operating room, no doubt, rescuing a hip joint. Not that he didn't love what he did. But this… other side of life in Marietta felt like he'd been hiding in his cave for a long time and just now could taste the fresh air.

He moved through the tables set with white tablecloths

and sprinkled with garlands and those red Christmas flowers he could never remember the name of that graced the perimeter of the grand room. But most of the tables had been abandoned for a turn on the dance floor, where all of Marietta seemed to be—dressed to the nines in their winter formal best.

At the far side of the room, he spotted Eve directing a burly pair of hotel employees to place a huge Christmas bouquet she'd borrowed from an inconspicuous place in the lobby to replace the late sugar plum fairy ice sculpture that had mysteriously broken. It didn't matter. The flowers looked meant to be and no one would be the wiser.

It was Eve he couldn't stop watching. In that dress of hers that looked cut to fit only her. In the dim lighting, her hair gleamed and his fingers itched to touch it again. Just remembering the kiss now had him breaking out into a sweat. All his careful arguments against getting involved with her had flown out the window tonight before he could think rationally about what he was doing. But only because he'd realized he was fighting a one-man battle. She was not fighting, despite their decision to keep things as they were. Nothing would remain static between them because, apparently, it could not. Theirs was an ever-evolving mess of a relationship that would only keep getting more complex the longer he stayed.

But he was leaving.

To the other side of the world.

To work he loved and wanted to do.

"Ben! Look at you!" Jake's voice came from nearby and he turned to find him and Olivia walking hand in hand toward the table. "It's not often we see you out of scrubs." They shook hands and Ben gave Olivia a kiss on the cheek. She was beautiful in a silvery floor-length gown that made her blue eyes even bluer.

"You can thank Eve," Ben said, running a finger under the collar of his shirt. "She's to blame for my being here."

"Where is she?" Olivia asked.

"Last minute emergency. She'll be right over."

At the table, Jaycee and Reed Canaday were sitting with Kate and her husband, Finn. Trey Reyes, Reed's law firm's P.I., shared the table with them, looking continental all decked out in a tux. It seemed safe to say that after Trey had single-handedly turned the tide in Finn's custody suit for his twins, he deserved his place at their table.

As Ben arrived, everyone stood to greet him. "Please, don't get up."

But he was welcomed like family to the table, just as he always was with this group. He had often wondered what it would be like to be part of a family like this one, where unconditional support and love was a given. He'd long ago moved past the need for such a thing, but when he was around the Canadays, he couldn't help but imagine what life would be like within their sphere.

"We hear you've taken a job down in Central America,"

Reed said as they all took seats around the table. "That's a real shame, Ben—and I'm speaking for us here, because we'll miss you—but I'm sure you'll do amazing work down there where it's greatly needed."

Uncomfortable with the topic, he nodded. "It's been on my radar for a while. Time for a change. Shake things up."

Finn said, "We were lucky you were here when Cutter broke his arm last fall. He still talks about that neon-green cast you put on him. And he's even been making noises about being a doctor someday."

"Which"—Kate interjected, touching Finn's arm—"is somewhat safer than sitting on top of a thousand pounds of angry bull."

"Hey, I'm all for it," Finn agreed.

Ben smiled, remembering Cutter who'd been brave in the face of a painful distal radius fracture.

"Jake tells me you and he used to ride horses together when you were kids up at the Sheenan place," Finn said to Ben. "So, you're a cowboy disguised as a doctor, eh?"

He laughed. "Not really, but I have to say, mucking out stalls at Malcolm's place brings back fond memories of my summers working at that ranch. I nearly became a veterinarian before fixing my sights on human beings."

"What's this about human beings?" Eve asked, sweeping up beside him with a smile.

Jaycee and Reed got up again to kiss and hug her hello. Everyone else followed suit.

Jake said, "Ben was just saying he liked horses almost better than people."

"A valid context," Finn agreed.

"Is that right?" Eve asked, grinning up at him.

Ben blushed, uncomfortable being the center of attention. Fortunately, Olivia jumped in to save him.

"Eve, this ballroom is exquisite and you have the magic touch."

"Aw, thanks. I think it turned out pretty well, minus one sugar plum fairy."

"Who?" Jaycee asked.

"Oh, nothing. Just a broken ice sculpture. Why aren't you all dancing? We can't just sit around at our table like a bunch of—"

"Cowboys?" Finn finished.

Eve laughed. "If I don't miss my guess, there will be line dancing when push comes to shove. Even cowboys do that. Besides, I've seen you dance, so don't try to pull the wool over my eyes, buster."

Kate pulled him up by the hand. "There. You've been put in your place. Now dance with me, cowboy!"

Without a trace of reluctance, Finn got up and steered her to the dance floor. Reed and Jaycee joined them after oohing and ahhing over the decorations to Eve for another minute. And Olivia and Jake left, too, heading over to snag champagne from a passing waiter.

"Well?" Eve said, folding her hands primly on the now

empty table. "Are you going to ask me to dance or not?"

"I warned you. My misspent youth did nothing for me on the dance floor."

"Did you see these shoes I'm wearing?" She lifted her skirts to point out her Louboutin's. "These are not the kind of shoes that stay tucked under a table. They can take whatever you can dish out on the dance floor."

"Fair enough," he agreed and tugged her up by the hand. "May I have this dance?"

"I thought you'd never ask."

The small orchestra of musicians and a singer, tucked into the fourth corner of the room, played a Christmas tune he couldn't name to which half the room was slow dancing. He led Eve out onto the floor, sure he would make a fool of himself tonight. But when he took her in his arms, she pressed herself up against him and guided him through the simple steps.

After a few minutes, he took the lead moving them incrementally around the dance floor between the crowds. Fortunately, the dancers were packed closely enough together no one could see if he stepped on her toes or if his technique sucked. For her part, Eve didn't seem to care. She smiled up at him as they moved together, then rested her head on his shoulder.

"I'm not a complete embarrassment, then?" he asked after a few moments of holding her close.

"I would dance with you any day," she said. "Why have

we never done this before on all of our friend dates?"

"Self-preservation," he admitted. "But now that we've broken the ice… I mean…."

She glanced up, but her gaze flickered quickly downward again. Now that they'd broken the ice, so to speak, they'd also run out of time.

A moment later, she asked, "How was your day with Lily?"

He glanced down at her, reminding her that he'd seen her earlier, standing on the balcony. "It was good. But I guess you saw that."

"Part of it," she admitted with an embarrassed smile. "You two looked good together."

"Yeah? She didn't have much of a Christmas list in mind when Santa asked her what she wanted. She just said she wanted her daddy to come home for Christmas."

"What did Santa say to that?"

"The poor guy looked up at me for help and I wasn't sure what to say. So I gave him a thumb's up."

"She's missing him terribly, I'm sure." Her hands tightened around him. "Let's hope Santa can come through for her this year."

"If all goes well, he should be out in a day or two. I took a look at his CT scans this afternoon and everything looks good."

"Thank God for small things. And the reindeer food?"

"Distributed and accounted for. A big hit with the children on the floor. Not so much for the nurses who will be cleaning up after those reindeer. But Lily liked it. She's still too young to process the whole hospital thing but she did ask why those children couldn't have Christmas at home."

"I think Patsy would have liked that you did that with her, today. In fact, I know she would have."

"Yeah." He hoped so, anyway. "Next on the list, Christmas caroling."

"You got another letter?"

"From Santa Claus himself. But there was a personal note for Malcolm in it so I took it to him."

Find someone to love.

And if he were the sort of man who believed in cosmic machinations or coincidence, he might actually imagine that Patsy was somehow speaking to him as well. But he didn't.

The song ended and couples applauded the singer with the big, bluesy voice. The president of the Daughters of Montana, a middle-aged woman he didn't know, gathered the daughters up on stage to welcome the guests and thank them for coming. This year's ball, she announced, was a benefit for the courthouse, in great need of renovation and all the profits collected for the ball would be going directly to that cause. The attorneys in the crowd, including Reed Canaday, applauded loudly for that and Eve joined in.

"Please also give a warm hand to our designer, Eve Canaday and her team, for making this ballroom look so fantastic! Isn't it beautiful? Eve? Where are you? Oh, there she is."

The room broke out in applause again.

Embarrassed, Eve leaned in to Ben. "Oh, God." But she waved a quick thank-you.

Afterward, with an admonishment to the crowd to enjoy themselves, the president turned the mic back over to the singer.

They danced to the next song, a waltz he didn't even really attempt, but instead, moved to the music with her in his arms.

"This place," he said, "it's really beautiful. This is all you."

"Oh, thanks," she murmured, "but I had a lot of help."

"Your vision."

She smiled up at him with that sexy confidence of hers. "It turned out pretty well, I think."

He had to agree. "With all the weddings going on in Marietta these days, your services will, no doubt, be in high demand."

"Actually, I'm doing Olivia and Jake's wedding this spring."

He spun her around as the band finished up the song. "They'll be lucky to have you."

"Too bad you won't be here for it. Jake will miss you there."

He'd forgotten about their upcoming wedding. Wrong of him to miss such an important date for his good friend.

Maybe he'd be able to fly back, and—

"Oh, my gosh," Eve gasped, oblivious to his self-recriminations. "Is that him?"

Following her line of sight, Ben said, "Who?"

"Prince Theodore Chenery, of course!"

At the other side of the room, a crowd was gathering around a newcomer to the fete, a tall, stately-looking guy who was handsome enough that he might've gotten lost from some Jane Austin novel, with women surrounding him. One woman in particular, who was clearly his date and shying back from the limelight.

"That's Rowan Palotay with him. Do you remember her? She was only a year ahead of me in school, but a few years behind you. To see her with a prince? Wow."

"You're impressed?"

"Well…" she prevaricated. "He is quite handsome, isn't he?"

If men who looked at home on red carpets were her thing, then he supposed so. Ben frowned, taking in the man across the room objectively. He wasn't so insecure he couldn't appreciate the appeal, but he didn't particularly enjoy watching Eve ogle the man. Was she actually standing on her tiptoes?

"Royalty in Marietta. What next?" Eve sighed dreamily.

"An invasion of phantom reindeer?"

She grinned, tugging him back in the direction of the table as waiters began filtering into the room carrying trays of food. “It’s not a phantom if we both saw it.”

“You know, I asked that petting zoo guy at the tree farm about missing a reindeer and he said he was the only one in town with reindeer. And he hadn’t lost one. And I keep hearing… bells.”

“Hmmm. Auditory hallucinations? You *are* getting in the spirit of Christmas.”

“Maybe I am,” he said with a grin.

They practically bumped into another couple on the dance floor and Ben introduced them to her. “Eve Canaday, this is Dr. Wyatt Gallagher and his friend—?”

The pretty woman with short, strawberry blonde hair leaned forward with a smile. “Mia Watson. Nice to meet you.”

Wyatt shook Eve’s hand. “Ben and I work together in ortho. He’s a terrific surgeon, you know.”

“I know. So nice meet you both.”

“You, too,” Mia said. “And beautiful job on this room. It’s stunning.”

Eve thanked them and they moved on. “They’re nice.”

Ben nodded his agreement.

“By the way, Ben, my parents always do a big Christmas Eve get together at their place at Lane’s End. We’ll be done at Malcolm’s by then. I hope you’ll come this year. Before you leave. I’d love it if you did.”

“I—” Feeling a little whiplashed by the question, he nodded. “I don’t usually *do* Christmas Eve.”

"But this year, you will. Because you're putting all that I-Hate-Christmas bullshit behind you, right?"

He laughed. "Don't hold back, Eve. Say what you really think."

"I will. I say it's time to put that old mythology to rest and create some of your own. Starting with celebrating with us. We all sing Christmas carols by the fire—some of us better than others—and eat amazing food and play greedy bingo until we run out of presents. And it's never just us, but also our extended family, all the people we think of as family. You included."

If he was capable of having a lump in his throat at such an invitation, one formed now. Put old mythology to rest? Was that what his life was? Just an old story that wasn't working for him anymore?

"Sure. I'd love to come," he said, before he could think any more about it. "Thanks. If you're sure I wouldn't be—"

"You wouldn't" she assured him. "Now, I think they're serving dinner over there, so we'd better get there before the family Canaday devours ours."

With an impish smile, she tugged him by the hand and headed to their table. He wasn't a man who followed much in his life. He was used to taking the lead, breaking the trail. But it occurred to him at that moment he was more than content to pin his gaze on her as she moved through the crowd, saying hellos as she went and leaving smiles in her wake. That was just who she was. Her talent for landscaping parties, arranging things into art, spilled over into the rest of her life. And damned if she hadn't managed to arrange his life, too.

Resistance was futile.

And he wasn't sure why he'd never really seen that before now.

THE CANADAYS SPENT the meal laughing and chatting, each of them catching up with the rest. Friends stopped by their table to say hello and a not a few of Eve's girlfriends cast questioning—okay, curious—looks at him in passing. Eve stayed mum about whatever was going on between them. No point in stirring up the gossip mills.

Trey Reyes, always the mystery man, seemed to be enjoying himself, though he rarely jumped in with an opinion or comment. So, Eve made it a point to engage him in a conversation about whale watching off the coast of Southern California, where he spent about half his time in Los Angeles and sometimes, Laguna Beach. He and Ben had common interests in scuba diving and Eve listened, fascinated, when they discussed the dive spots they loved best.

When the conversation took a weird turn to internet privacy, something both of them were concerned with in their private businesses, Eve's ears perked up. Being a private investigator, Trey knew more than most about such things, particularly about internet security.

"So on that topic," she said, "how hard is it to find a person's personal information on the internet. I mean, just randomly."

"Shockingly easy," Trey acknowledged. "Give me a name, I'll have their address, phone number and their last year's income before you could dial their phone to warn them."

"*Really.*" Eve's mind panned backward to all the weirdos who'd intersected her life she hoped would never find her.

"Why do you ask?"

She fiddled with her fork. "Well, someone came to my door tonight, wanting to give me a resume for a job I advertised in the *Courier*. I never mentioned my home address, obviously."

"It might take more hutzpah than skill to do that," he said. "You worried about it?"

A little. "Oh, no. No. But her hutzpah won't land her the job. I guarantee you that."

"You're tough," Ben said, teasingly. "What if she's just really hungry for work? Or really good?"

She shrugged. "I'm really not tough. Just cautious. But now that Trey has scared me silly," she said, distractedly, watching the very handsome prince spin his date across the dance floor, "I may need to get a man—" Her eyes widened. "I-I mean a *dog*—I mean a *male* dog."

Good God. Her cheeks went hot and she counted backward from ten.

For his part, Ben covered the lower half of his jaw with his hand and squinted at her.

"Want another drink?" he asked, lifting her empty wine glass. "I could use one."

"Yes, please. As soon as humanly possible."

"Be right back." Ben left the table and headed for the bar set up across the room.

She couldn't imagine what he was thinking. Probably that he should run as far and as fast as he could from her brand of crazy.

Trey grinned at her. "Dog's a good idea."

"Ugh!" She dropped her head into her hands. "Just shoot me now."

"If it didn't matter to him, it wouldn't make him nervous."

"Don't try to make me feel better."

"Okay," Trey said, sipping his scotch with a chuckle.

"But tell me this." Eve sent him a beseeching look. "Are all men as complicated as you and Ben?"

"Me? How'd I get in the middle of this?"

"Sorry. I just mean, you quiet ones, you know? You're hard to figure out."

He sent her an enigmatic smile. "Maybe you got it backwards. Maybe he's trying to figure you out."

"And ever rivers will cross…" she muttered.

Except his river was about to be somewhere in Honduras and she was pretty sure there wasn't any river nearby that would intersect with that one.

At least, for the past year, she'd been able to pretend they had some possible future together. If that potential still lingered in her mind, despite the kiss tonight, it was her bad. Nothing had changed, really, except the way he'd been looking at her since their kiss. But for a man like Ben, a man with places to go, things to accomplish, that look only meant he would think of her on some lonely night in the jungle somewhere and wonder what she was up to. It didn't mean he would stay.

No one gets out unscathed.

Especially her.

Kate and Finn returned from the dance floor and her sister leaned in to her. "Well?"

"Well, what?"

"How's it going with you two?"

"Fine," she said, her gaze tracking him across the room.

"I'd say it's a little better than fine. Second opinion, Trey. There's something going on between these two, don't you think?"

Trey kindly demurred, sipping his scotch. "I make it a policy never to interpret. I only collect facts."

"How diplomatic of you," Kate said. "But facts are, he hasn't taken his eyes off you all night."

Except to roll them, maybe. Eve hadn't told her about the kiss they'd shared earlier. She wanted to keep it private. Once her family got wind of it, they'd come to all sorts of wrong conclusions. But if she and Ben could capture at least this small bit of time they had left, and be happy, why shouldn't they? Time enough later for broken hearts. And long distance regrets. They'd be there anyway, full force, once he left.

"Have you talked to Izzy tonight?" she asked Kate. "How are the kids doing?"

"They're all fine. Sleeping on the floor in Caylee's room together. We promised them pancakes in the morning if they were good for Izzy, so of course, they were up until nine. Lily seemed thrilled to be part of it." She glanced around the room. "I need to freshen up my lipstick. Come with me?"

Happy for an excuse to move, Eve nodded. They made their way through the tables to the restroom where the lounge was nearly empty.

Kate pulled out her lipstick, but watched Eve in the mirror. "I haven't told anyone else yet, but Finn and I… we're pregnant."

Eve fumbled her lipstick. "What? Oh, my God! Kate!" She hadn't even paid attention to the fact that Kate had been drinking nothing but water all night. She threw her arms around her and hugged her tight.

"I know," Kate whispered. "We're really happy about it. I wasn't going to tell you yet, but since things seem to be going well for you two…."

"Forget *me*. That's fantastic news, Kate. How far along are you?"

"Barely three months. I'm due in June."

"How are you feeling? Have you been sick?"

"No. Not at all. I feel great," she said.

"So… you'll be pregnant for Olivia's wedding."

"In all my bridesmaid splendor."

"I cannot wait to see your pregnant belly and I cannot wait to see the child you and Finn make together."

Kate squeezed her hands. "Me, too. I'll tell everyone after Christmas, so keep it on the down low, okay?"

Eve zipped her lips and turned the imaginary key. "Thank you for telling me. I needed to hear something spectacular tonight."

"You know, less than a year ago" Kate said, "it looked like it would never happen for me and Finn. But here we are. About to add to our little family. I'm keeping my fingers and toes crossed for you guys."

Back to Ben. "Thanks, but you know he's leaving, right? He's given notice and everything. He's not going to change his mind."

"Never say never. Okay," Kate said. "I said it was a lipstick run, but truthfully? I have to pee. I have to pee all the time these days."

Eve laughed. "Okay. I'll meet you back at the table."

But she went to go find Ben.

THE LINE FOR drinks was longer than he'd expected and he

was nearly at the bar when a woman spoke behind him.

"I could take you anywhere in that tux."

He turned. Kimberly Trask, out of her pharmaceutical rep designer suit and dressed in a very expensive-looking blue number that brushed the floor, was standing a little too close for comfort.

"Hello, Kimberly."

"Hello, yourself. You're looking very handsome tonight."

"Thanks. You, too." She did, but he was only being polite.

He didn't want to engage her.

"Mind if I cut in?" She glanced back at the middle-aged man waiting behind Ben, asking permission with a flirty little smile. "I'm *so* thirsty."

"Go right ahead," the man said, flirting right back. "I'm in no hurry."

Ben gritted his teeth as she wedged herself between that man and him in line.

"So I had to settle for my second choice to bring me here tonight," she murmured. "Dr. Rigby. Plastics?" Rigby was fifty, divorced, and, famously, a womanizer. Kimberly scanned the crowd purposefully. "Who's your friend?" She turned back to him. "You did say you were bringing a friend, didn't you?"

Ben flicked an irritated look back at the man behind them who was listening intently to the whole conversation. "I'm here with Eve Canaday."

"Oh. That designer girl? That's sweet and very generous of you."

"Not generous at all. I'm the lucky one."

"Ahh. How gallant. You know, I heard a rumor about you."

He inched forward in line, contemplating giving up on the drink thing altogether. "Oh?"

"Someone told me you're leaving Marietta. For ex-pat work. Is that true?"

He had no desire to discuss his plans with her. "And I heard you were one of the top reps in your company this year."

A pleased flush crept up her cheeks and she laughed. "You did? Who told you that?"

"I can't recall." He'd never actually heard that, but he flashed a smile at her, relieved her narcissism could work to his advantage. "I heard it somewhere."

"I'm always looking to improve my stats," she murmured close to his ear. "So, are you leaving?"

He reached the front of the line just then. "Two cabernets please."

"Because, if you are," she continued, leaning closer, "that might break my heart." She looked up deliberately. "Oh, look, mistletoe!"

Sure enough, directly over the bar was a giant ball of mistletoe.

And when he looked back, Kimberly planted a kiss on

him. Hard. Right there in front of the bartender, the bug-eyed guy behind them, and everyone in the room. He was so surprised, it took him a second before he could tug her arms down and hold her away from him. He didn't want to make a scene, of which she was more than capable of managing all on her own.

"That's enough," he warned her quietly.

She ran the tip of her finger over her damp lips and *tisked.* "It was just a mistletoe kiss. That's what it's for, after all. It's tradition. No harm, no foul."

That was when he looked over her shoulder and saw Eve, frozen in place, staring at him in wide-eyed horror, a few dozen feet away.

Shit.

Eve whirled away, heading directly for the exit.

Ben dropped Kimberly's arm, glancing around him, catching the attention of half a dozen others who were already drawing their own conclusions. He went after Eve.

"It was just for fun," Kimberly called after him. "Ben?"

Chapter Ten

AAAAND, POOF!

Damn him for proving her right.

Eve couldn't get through the crowds fast enough. Yet she seemed to collide with every partygoer on the way as she fought back tears.

He caught up with her at the coat check room and took her arm. "Eve. Wait. It's not what you think."

"No? I'm not blind, Ben. I don't know what sort of idiot you think I am, but—"

He searched his pocket for his own check ticket. "It was the mistletoe. She kissed *me*."

"Oh, Please. Don't insult me." *And don't let me slap him.*

The coat check girl handed her the wrap, eyeing the anger between them warily. Eve slipped her a few dollars and stalked toward the main doors. Her Louboutin's clacked against the lobby floor, past Santa's empty throne and the little paper clock that promised, "Be Back Soon!"

And to think. Just this afternoon, she'd been watching him with Lily, thinking her heart might break. And now it had!

Ben abandoned his coat and hurried after her. "Okay, that sounds lame, I know. But I had no intention of kissing her."

"Or me, either, so I guess Miss Mistletoe and I are even," she said, pulling out her phone to order a taxi. "Yes," she said when the cab company answered. "The Graff Hotel, please. I'm out front."

"What are you doing? You're not leaving here without me."

"Yes, I am."

"No." He gestured to the valet and handed him his parking ticket. "Fast, please. Eve, listen to me—"

She whirled on him. "You not only kissed her, you kissed her in front of the entire town of Marietta, and my family, when everyone knew you came here with me! It's not bad enough I had to beg you to take me. Did you have to humiliate me, too?"

He growled a low curse. "I'm sorry. Dammit, I'm so sorry. I never meant for that to happen. I sure as hell never meant to humiliate you."

"No, I'm sure you thought I'd never see it. But I did. And I can't unsee it." Tears blurred her vision and she blinked them away.

"I wasn't going behind your back. It was nothing like that. Kimberly—"

"Oh, I know who she is. Every wife of every doctor in

town knows who she is. People talk, you know."

Ben lowered his head. "It wasn't like that."

"Maybe any pair of lips would suffice for you tonight," she shot back, feeling self-righteous as she scanned the dark for signs of the cab driver.

"You know that's not true." He gestured at the phone. "Call them back. Cancel the car. I'm taking you home."

"No."

He snagged her phone and did it for her as she tried to snatch it back. "Stop it, Ben!"

The valet returned with his car and it came screeching up to the curb.

He yanked the passenger door open. "Get in."

"No."

Even as she said it, two couples exited the hotel behind them, heading for the valet stand a few feet away. Carol Bingley, the town gossip, was one of them. The mayor and his wife were there, too.

"You want to make more of a scene? No? Then just get in, Eve."

She glared at him, furious, then plopped herself down in the passenger seat.

Ben came around the other side and slid into the driver's seat. He took off, leaving the Graff Hotel and her triumphant disaster of a night behind them. She hadn't even told her family goodbye.

"I need my phone back."

Reluctantly, he handed the thing to her. She texted Kate a brief message, then stared blindly out the window as the town's Christmas lights sped past them.

"Take me to my place," she told him.

"We're going to go back to Malcolm's and talk first. Then, if you still want to go home, I'll take you."

"No! Talk about what? The kiss? You and Kimberly? I don't want to talk about that. I don't want to talk at all."

"I understand you're upset—"

"That's just it. I don't really think you do understand."

"I do. I know it looked bad. But—"

"Looked bad?" She laughed without humor, turning on him with tears in her eyes. "It didn't just look bad, Ben. How about humiliating? You can't possibly think you can do something like that—let Kimberly Trask hang all over you at the ball you brought me to and think I wouldn't react! You're not actually that clueless, are you?" She shook her head. "Oh. Maybe you are."

His knuckles whitened on the steering wheel. "Kimberly kissed *me*."

She made a face. "One thing I never took you for was a coward, Ben."

His expression darkened. "What's that supposed to mean?"

"Blaming Kimberly for that kiss is like… like… blaming a puppy for peeing on the floor. That's who that woman is. If you didn't know what Kimberly had in mind when she sidled up to you in that line, in front of my family and friends, then you're definitely not as smart as you think you are. But frankly, I think you let it happen." Against her will, tears leaked out of the corners of her eyes.

"*What*?"

She turned a laser beam of anger on him. "Well, let's face it, Ben, that's your M.O. isn't it? Things get a little too close and you head for the hills? Or Honduras. Or Kimberly. Whatever."

"That's not fair." Ben scowled at the beam of lights that tunneled through the night ahead of them as he pulled down the road to Malcolm's house and headed up the driveway.

Of course she was mad, as she had every right to be mad. He just had to figure out how to fix this.

"Really? We're gonna talk fair now? Like we're six? Okay. Is it fair that I care about you and all you want to do is run away from me? Or that, despite our friendship, you lied to me about going? Or that you think you can sneak out of your part in that whole charade back there by saying it was her fault and expect it's no big deal. '*Oops! My bad. What? You're mad*?'"

"I can see very plainly that you're mad. But this isn't just about the kiss, is it? This is about everything. About *me*."

"Maybe it is." She sank back in her seat and turned her face from him. "Maybe it's about us. Which is an oxymoron, since there really is no 'us.'"

His chest tightened with an old wound that just seemed

to keep festering. And even though he saw the damned wound for what it was, he couldn't seem to move past it. Had he really sabotaged them himself with that fuck up with Kimberly by allowing that kiss to happen? She was right. Of course he'd known Kimberly was up to no good. What male wouldn't know? She'd had her sights on him for months now. But to say he meant to hurt Eve intentionally…

Eve sniffled. "And you know what's really pathetic? I've waited a year for you to kiss me the way you did tonight. For you to even notice I was here. And when you finally did, it turns out that it really meant nothing to you."

"That's just not true."

"Yeah, it is. It was just another kiss. One even Kimberly, the pharma rep, could manage without groveling."

Stunned by her words, his mind whirred, remembering a thousand looks from Eve he had missed, her smiles, the trust she'd put in him, the hopeful brightness in her eyes. These things flashed before him now like a pinwheel, like a movie reel of mistakes he'd made with her, all of which she'd given him a pass on. Until now.

He pulled the car to a stop in front of Malcolm's house and Eve sat for a moment in silence. Then she opened the door and stalked toward the house without him. He got out and followed her in, closing the door behind them as quietly as he could.

Inside, the flip of a switch turned on the Christmas tree lights—the tree they'd decorated together—and cast the room in a glow that had no place in what was going on with them right now.

Eve tugged the fur wrap closer around her and held it, like she had no intention of staying. "Nothing?" she asked quietly. "You have nothing more to say?"

"Obviously, sorry is insufficient. And if you're right about me—which, apparently you are—that makes me an ass. And why would you want a part of that anyway?" He moved to the fireplace where he hit the switch to ignite the gas logs, because he wanted something else to stare at instead of the accusation in her eyes.

"Don't you try to make me feel sorry for you. Not tonight. Not when I'm… I'm standing in my indignation. You'd better damn well take it if you care about me at all."

God, was he doing that? He turned back to her. "You're right. But I don't know how to fix this."

She shook her head a little sadly. "You know what your problem is, Ben?"

"No," he said, feeling resentful that someone had to spell it out for him. "Why don't you tell me."

"You think you can fix everything in a nice, neat little package and still keep your distance. Maybe you can just wrap this all up before you go, right? Before your sojourn to Honduras? Spit, spat! Brush your hands together and move on. Don't allow yourself to see things for what they really are. Because real life isn't like your world in medicine, Ben, where you have to constantly protect yourself from feeling too deeply about your patients." She shook her head in frustration.

"You've been in medicine so long you've forgotten how the real world works. Here, in this-is-your-life-world, you can't step away from all of your feelings and pretend you can live without them. Because you can't. Not really. Not fully. And there's another person in this equation." She flattened a palm over her chest. "*I* have feelings, too. My feelings matter. And just because you don't consider my feelings when you're deciding to protect yourself, doesn't mean I don't matter. Or that my feelings aren't just as important as yours." Tears rolled down her cheeks, falling on the fake fur wrap around her shoulders.

Ahhh! Hell, he'd made such a mess of tonight. And still, he wanted to make excuses. Say she wasn't right about him. Tell her she was off base about his intentions. But she was right about one thing—he'd chosen medicine intentionally, like a moat around his life. Protecting him from this very thing. And just maybe he'd been too busy filling the damned thing with water to notice her drowning a few feet away.

He pushed away from the mantle and moved toward her. Chin up, she took an evasive step back and he stopped a few feet away from her.

"I hurt you," he said softly. "I'm flawed. Okay? Deeply flawed. And the optics tonight, no matter what the intention, were bad. That's on me. I fucked up. And I'm truly, deeply sorry, Eve. But you're wrong if you think I *wanted* to hurt you. I didn't. I never would."

She watched him, wiping her cheek with a palm. "Things you do have consequences, Ben. Whether they're intentional or not." She turned away.

"I know." His whole life felt like a consequence right now.

A deepening hole that sprang from all the fucked up things he'd done to spare himself pain. And none of that had worked. None of it.

"Why didn't you ever tell me how you felt?" he asked softly.

"I just didn't. It felt too… risky. I guess I was waiting for a sign. From the universe. Stupid me. I thought this time with Lily was it. When I hung those mistletoe balls, I was hoping it would be me you'd be kissing underneath them. But we have no claim on each other. You can kiss whomever you want. And so can I. Anyway, what difference would it have made if I had told you? You probably would have just laughed at me."

He sent her a pained look. "No. I wouldn't have. Not at all."

"You were too busy fending off nurses and pharma reps to bother with me."

There was real sadness in her voice and he hated he'd put it there.

"I was trying to hold onto what we had. What we could keep. Our friendship, at least."

"That's just an excuse." She turned back to him and looked up at him through her dark lashes. "What's wrong with us Ben, that we can't just be honest with each other? I'm tired of talking around the truth. Life is too short for that. Here we are, in Patsy's house and that loss seems to have taught us nothing."

He stepped over to her and took her by the shoulders. "Except this. The only person I wanted to kiss in that whole place tonight was you. Only you."

"Oh, Ben…" She stiffened in his arms, but he didn't let her go.

"It was you I wanted to kiss under that mistletoe, press you hard up against me and pretend—if only for tonight—that I was enough for you."

She opened her mouth to speak, but he went on, cupping the back of her head with his hand, digging his fingers into her hair. "Because all I've been able to think about since we started this whole Lily thing is how you make me better. You make me feel things, Eve. God—you do. And I'm no good at that. That's pretty clear, right? I'm not particularly good with words either, like you are. But I will tell you this." His fingers spread across her back underneath that little fur thing of hers and he dropped his forehead against hers. "If I could take this night back, hell—this year—and start again, I would do it differently with you."

"But you can't." Her whispered words were stark.

"No. I can't." He kissed her closed eyes, her cheek, the

tender spot beside her mouth. "You'll just have to believe me when I say… I hear you. You're right about me." He kissed her throat.

"Don't… don't say what you don't mean."

He slammed his eyes shut. "Forgive me, Eve. You have to forgive me. We can't leave it this way."

"You shouldn't be kissing me."

"It's all I've got." He dropped his mouth onto hers and kissed her for real, swirling his tongue against hers in a hungry, desperate apology.

Her mouth slanted against his, first one way, then the other and he pulled her flush against him and felt her knees sway.

Lifting her mouth from his, she breathed, "I shouldn't… I shouldn't be letting you."

But he captured hers again and kissed her until he ran out of air and heard her gasping, too. Blindly, his fingers found the clasp on her wrap and undid it, pushing it out of his way. He slid it off her shoulders, exposing her bare arms and the low-cut bodice of her gown. *Ahh.* He wanted her. He wanted all of her. Wanted to make up for all the wrongs he'd done to her.

Yet the tumble of hunger in his gut waged a searing battle with what remained of his ethics. Because sex with Eve now would only prove her right about him.

But they had backed up against the table and now, she nearly fell backward before he caught her and lowered her down against it while she kissed him. Breaking the kiss, he stared down at her in the dim light, marveling at the feelings she evoked in him. Unfamiliar, foreign emotions that somehow felt as natural as breathing when he was with her.

"If you don't forgive me," he whispered, pressing his lips against her soft cheek, "I'll have to make love to you. Right here. Right now. And that would be—"

"—a mistake. Wouldn't it?" She slid her eyes shut with frustration. "Oh, I don't know what I'm doing anymore. You make me... crazy." With a shake of her head, she whispered, "Damn you, Ben Tyler."

"Too late for that."

She shut him up by pulling him down for an angry kiss, hard against his mouth. Their teeth scraped together in the franticness of the kiss, and she bit his lip—not hard, but hard enough to sting him.

"*That's* for Kimberly."

Her eyes darkened as he met her gaze, touching his lip with his tongue. With a jerk on the end of his bow tie, he undid the thing and flicked open the collar on his starched, white shirt before taking her mouth again. His hands roved down the sides of her ribs while hers went around his back, the over-warm fabric of his tux jacket a boundary he wished was gone. But never mind. He had more important things to attend to, like memorizing the feel of her lips on his, the delicious friction of her breasts against his chest, the way she felt like she belonged in his arms.

Her tongue slid against his and he felt her soften beneath him, her body relaxing against his, sinking into the kiss and into his arms.

And before he lost it altogether, using every bit of restraint he could muster, he broke the kiss and brushed a strand of hair gently from her eyes. "Does that mean you accept my apology?"

She arched her back with a sigh, studying him for a long moment while weighing her answer. Finally, her mouth twisted in a small sign of surrender. "Fine. Yes," she said, watching him through her lashes, "but this table's really hard. And I think I'm lying on a cranberry."

He grinned and reluctantly took his weight off her, pulling her up by one hand to a sit. She cracked her neck as she straightened her skirts just as someone began banging on the front door.

Eve jumped, clutching her dress and hopping off the dining table with a guilty flush. "Who could that be?"

"Ben?" A voice called from outside. "It's Jonas. You in there?"

Like guilty teenagers, caught by their parents, he and Eve stared at each other in shocked silence. If he looked anything like her, the flush of their kisses still lingered on his face.

"Be right there, Jonas!" he called, motioning Eve into the next room before swinging open the front door. "Jonas?"

"Oh. Ben. Thank God. I saw your car when I came out of the barn. I didn't realize you were home. Miranda's in labor and she's having a lot of trouble. I think the foal's breech. I can't get hold of the vet, Dr. Seamis. He must be at that shindig in town."

"He could be."

"I have to drive over there, try to find him. I've left messages but he's not looking at his phone. Can you sit with the mare while I'm gone?"

"You say she's breech?"

"I'm a cattle guy, not a horse guy, but I've seen this before and it's not good. I'd hate to lose Malcolm's foal. Not now, after everything that's happened to him. I hoped maybe your doctoring skills would come in handy."

"How long has she been laboring?"

"Don't know for sure. I got here an hour ago to check on her before turning in and she was lying down, having trouble."

"Okay. You go see if you can find the vet. I'll do what I can."

Jonas nodded and hurried back to his truck.

Ben turned to Eve who reappeared beside him. "Go change out of that pretty dress. I might need your help."

She nodded. "I'll be right out."

EVE HURRIED INTO the barn a few minutes later, dressed in jeans and a shirt, marveling at the turns this night had taken already. Ben had already shed his tux jacket and was stripping his shirt off.

The sight of his bare torso sent a new ripple of heat through her and she blinked. This was not the time to be thinking about such things, though she had barely had time to recover from what had just happened between them. A blush heated her cheeks as he looked up at her, heat still lingering in his eyes as well. But just as quickly, he turned back to the mare, all business again.

The mare was laboring hard and making noises that indicated she was struggling. And there seemed to be nothing yet to show for all her trouble.

"What are you going to do?"

"Check her."

She knew exactly what that meant. "Be careful, Ben. Those contractions are strong enough to break bones. Don't risk your hands."

"I don't see much choice. But my only experience with childbirth was during my obstetrics rotation. That and seeing a couple foals born when I was a kid. If she's breech, I'm not sure that foal has time to wait for the vet, especially if the cord is constricted. But I could use a bar of soap and warm water if there's any to be had."

She nodded and went to look. When she returned with the bucket and soap, Ben was kneeling beside Miranda running his hands over her belly. "My guess, the head is turned. Stuck. You want to help?"

That was not good.

With a nod, she said, "Of course."

"Sit up here at her head and try to keep her calm and lying down."

Eve settled beside the horse in the straw, watching Ben soap up his arm to the shoulder.

Nothing about what he was doing was easy, from the inherent danger of his position, to the compression of his arm caused by the contractions. Miranda suffered through contractions that made no obvious progress and she didn't seem to even have the wherewithal to protest Ben's interference.

"The head should be delivered parallel to the legs," Eve said. "And if it's turned sideways, there's no way that foal is coming out."

He sent a surprised look her way.

"I was raised around horses." She reminded him with a shrug. "I do know a thing or two about them."

Minutes passed. She kept talking to the mare, calming her as he reached inside her for the foal. But, after what seemed like hours, but was probably only minutes, he found the foal's outstretched legs and encountered the problem. "Got it. I'm gonna try to turn her head. Keep her still."

"I've got her," she assured him, holding the mare's halter and brushing a calming palm down her forehead. "No getting up now, Miss Miranda. Stay right where you are."

He grimaced and sucked in a breath as if a boa constrictor had him by the arm. His muscles strained, and a fine sheen of sweat covered his chest and arms, despite the chilly air.

"Can you feel her muzzle?"

"My arm is… going… numb," he said, panting with the effort. "But… I think I'm almost… there. I can't tell if the foal is still alive. I can't feel it moving."

Malcolm had told them how important this foal was to him. But, regardless, the prospect of losing this baby, at full term, sent a chill down her.

Her parents had horses out at Lane's End and her sister, Olivia, was a world-class equestrian. Eve loved horses and rode whenever she could, but couldn't imagine doing what Ben was doing right now. She preferred to stay as far from the hooves of a mare in labor as humanly possible.

Ben's handsome face was a study in concentration. This was the man who stood for hours at a stretch over operating tables, determined to fix someone broken. Saving a life. This was his essence, his mission. And she was upset about losing him to a higher cause and worried about a kiss under a ball of mistletoe. All of that seemed to pale now in the face of this moment.

Squeezing his eyes shut again, he reached deeper. "There! There it is. Got it. Now if I can… just…"

With supreme effort, he slowly, slowly tugged the foal's muzzle around. "C'mon, baby," he whispered against Miranda's flanks. "Get out of there."

"Good girl," Eve cooed close to the mare's ear. "Thatta

girl. You can do it. Now push!"

No sooner had he turned the foal than the mare used what little strength she had left to push it out in a rush. The baby fell out onto the straw. It lay motionless.

"Oh, no! Ben!" Eve cried, emotion welling in her eyes. "Is she—?"

Ben cut open the sac surrounding the foal's nose and ripped it off her face. "Come on, breathe!"

He rubbed the foal's face and neck vigorously. Nothing.

Cupping his hands around the baby's nostrils, he blew hard, then started chest compressions. He repeated that for about thirty seconds. Eve sent up a prayer.

The mare finally gathered up the strength to roll to one side to see her baby. She sniffed at the motionless foal.

"Breathe!" Ben growled, striking the foal on the chest with his fist.

"Go on." Eve encouraged the mare. "Help your baby."

The mare gave a tentative lick to the foal's face, then another.

Miraculously, the foal twitched and sucked in a breath. Then another. She opened her eyes and blinked.

Miranda nickered at the foal and curled toward it to lick her face in earnest.

"Oh, man." Ben fell back against the stall wall, with an exhausted but triumphant smile.

"You saved her, Ben. You saved her life."

Still breathing heavily, he corrected, "We. We saved her

together. And that was a lot closer than I'd hoped for." Together, they watched her for a few quiet minutes, marveling at her miniature perfection. "She's still a little floppy. She's been through an ordeal and needs to feed to get her strength."

Eve shook her head. "She has to make it."

The foal kicked her legs then folded them under her, still looking fragile and astounded at the world in which she'd arrived.

Ben got to his feet and staggered toward the doorway. "I hope so. If she gets to her feet, we're golden. We should get out of her way, let Miranda take care of the foal now." Already, the mare was licking the baby all over.

Eve joined him at the stall door. "That was something, Ben. Good instincts."

He just smiled at her as he tugged a hand towel from a hook outside the stall and soaked it in the bucket before wiping the muck from his arm. "Science. Basic anatomy. A little CPR thrown in for good measure."

She nodded, going along. "Nothing magic about it. No coincidence that we were here at the right time, right place to save that little girl."

"Luck. That's all." His gaze slid down her as he washed off his arm. "I'm not really a big believer in—"

"I know. In cosmic machinations."

Miranda maneuvered herself around closer to her foal, who was already trying to stand, but couldn't quite manage it.

The foal had her dam's coloring, but for a white diamond-shaped patch on her brow. She looked more grasshopper than foal with those long legs splayed in all directions, trying to find her feet. "This never gets old, does it? Birth. Beginnings?" Eve said, smiling at the baby.

"Apparently, you must have seen your share of horses born out at Lane's End."

"A few. Olivia did some breeding and training when she was younger and we all loved watching them grow. I adore riding. I do it whenever I can. Now that Olivia's back up on horseback, we sometimes go for long rides up into the mountains. Maybe you'd like come sometime with—" she began, but stopped, remembering they were running out of time for any things they hadn't gotten to yet.

Suddenly self-conscious, she looked away.

In all the excitement of the birth, she'd forgotten their argument. Truth was, the kiss had merely been the trigger. There seemed to be a much more important issue here than who kissed whom at the ball.

Outside, she heard tires crunch on gravel and the sound of a two vehicles pulling into the yard. Ben straightened and a moment later, Malcolm's vet, Howard Seamis hurried through the barn door. Still dressed in a tux and an overcoat from the ball, he was carrying his medical bag. Jonas was right behind him.

Ben held up one hand. "Take it easy. It's all right. She's

okay. Miranda's got herself a little girl."

Seamis sagged at the stall door with relief. "Oh, thank God. But Jonas told me she was breech."

"She was." Ben quickly explained what had happened. Even as he did, the mare lurched upright and the little foal struggled to her feet as well, wobbling toward her mother's teat.

Seamis clapped Ben on the shoulder and joked, "If you ever consider changing careers… I might have an opening in my practice."

"I'll stick with humans, thanks," Ben said with a charming grin. "But I must admit, delivering this foal alive was gratifying. And I couldn't have done it without Eve keeping Miranda calm."

"Good work, both of you," Seamis said. "Somehow, I missed Jonas's calls, but when I finally saw his message, I jumped in the car. We met virtually halfway, and he turned around and followed me back. I would have never forgiven myself if anything had gone wrong with this foal. Poor Malcolm's had enough heartache this year without that."

"That's the truth." Jonas handed Ben his shirt. "You must be freezing, man."

"Nah," he said, but taking the shirt all the same. "Must be the adrenaline." But his gaze cut to Eve with a look so heated she felt dampness break out above her lip. She slid her gaze away.

"You three have done enough for one night. I'll take it

from here. Let me just check them both out and if everything is fine, I'll leave the foal to her mother's care. But I'll come back out first thing tomorrow. Just to be safe."

"All right. Goodnight, then," Ben said, taking Eve's hand in his. "Thanks for everything, Jonas. Dr. Seamis."

Once they got back to the house, they stood in the dark kitchen for a moment without speaking. What had happened earlier here lingered between them.

He said, "I'm a mess. I need a quick shower. You must be tired, but will you wait right here for me?"

She nodded. "I'll make us some hot tea."

"Good. I'll be right back."

She managed to slam down a half a glass of wine to brace her nerve for the conversation to come. His very sexy "apology" notwithstanding, she wasn't so sure anything had really changed between them. Would he want things to go further? Should she allow them to? Or, if she refused, was she simply letting herself in for more pain or closing the door on the possibility she could keep him in Marietta if things worked out between them.

One thing she knew. And she knew it through personal experience. Change could only come from within a person, not from anything another person did or tried to do to affect that change. If he was still set on running, leaving her here in Marietta, then he would go. And nothing that had already happened or might still happen, would change that.

And if she believed in herself enough to let him go, then

maybe that was her answer.

He broke records showering and was back as she put the tea to steep, looking slick and shiny clean with a towel draped around his neck. He had on his favorite pair of sweats again and a tee-shirt that tugged at the smooth, taut muscles of his chest.

She, on the other hand, still smelled like hay and horses. *Typical.*

Pulling a couple of mugs down from Malcolm's cupboard, she asked, "Better?"

"Much." He leaned a hip against the counter beside her and ran the damp towel over tousled hair.

She tried not to watch. And failed miserably. "About before—" she began, but faltered into silence.

"About before," he repeated. "I know it wasn't much of an apology."

"Oh"—she allowed, feeling a flash of heat at the memory—"it was a pretty good one. As apologies go. But I'm still not sure where that leaves us."

"What if…" he began, turning toward the window to stare out into the darkness, "what if you came to Honduras with me?"

"What?" She looked at him like he was crazy in the window's reflection.

He turned back to her. Took her by the arms, as if this spur of the moment idea was generating its own steam. "Come with me. It'll be an adventure."

She could tell he really believed what he was saying. That going there would be a high adventure, just like the rest of his life had been, with no promises, no security. No risk—for him, anyway.

She exhaled a weary laugh. "No, Ben. I'm not going to Honduras with you on some wild escapade. This is my home. This is where my family and my friends are. My business is here. I love it in Marietta. And I'm not running off to some jungle to… to explore possibilities with you."

He frowned. "That's not how I meant it."

"How did you mean it?"

"I meant to say, I want… I want…"

"What?"

"I want *us* to be more."

They were almost exactly the words she'd waited to hear from him. "Then stay."

"I can't."

And just like that, her hopes crashed and burned. "You *won't*."

He slammed his eyes shut. "I'm committed to go."

She wouldn't cry again. Not tonight. Already this seesaw of emotions he'd put her on was wearing her down.

"Then you should go. And leave me be." Eyes welling, she turned away, but he spun her back by the shoulders and kissed her.

He took her mouth so tenderly, with so much pent-up emotion, she forgot to breathe. Almost against her will, she slid her arms around him, holding on lest she fall. He backed her against the counter, shoving his hands into her hair on either side of her face. His fingers cradled her skull as if he couldn't get close enough, slanting his mouth first one way, then the other while his tongue danced with hers.

But somehow, she managed to work up the strength to stop it. Drag herself from him and stop it. "Don't. I think it's best if I go. Tonight."

"No," he pleaded. "Eve—"

She nodded. "I respect you, Ben, and what you want to do with your life. And you should go and do it, whatever that is. But it won't be with me. And honestly, if I stayed here tonight, we'd probably only make things worse between us, either by making love or fighting again. And right now, both of those things sound like disasters to me."

"Okay. All right." He held his hands up in surrender. "I won't touch you again. We won't fight. But don't go. Lily's coming home in the morning. I know she expects to see you. She needs you." He didn't say "and so do I". But it was there in his expression.

Relenting, she nodded. She didn't want to disappoint Lily. One more day was the least she could do for her. But somehow, she would have to survive it.

Suddenly, she was tired. Bone tired.

Chapter Eleven

THEY ROSE LONG after the sun came up and made breakfast, sharing food but little talk. He knew she was afraid of what he'd say and he feared the same thing. There were no recriminations about what had happened last night in the dining room. No more apologies. They were adults and fully aware of the implications of what had happened between them. But even as they readied for the day, he could feel her moving away from him. Distancing her heart from him. She was right to do it. He couldn't blame her. But neither could he do the same.

Kate dropped Lily off and they both came out to visit the newborn foal. Lily clung to Eve's side, holding her hand as she watched the foal nurse. She was quiet for a long time before she said, "I think we should name her Angel."

"That's a beautiful name, Lily. I'm sure your dad will love it." Eve met Ben's eyes then, over Lily's head, and he smiled at her, a smile tinged with all the heartbreak of a little girl who'd lost her mother. And a man who'd lost his center.

After the vet came to check on the foal, he and Lily and

Eve headed back to the house. Eve promised to make snow angels with her in the yard.

"I'm going to go check on Malcolm," he said when Lily ran off to her room to find her snow pants. "You okay here by yourself for a little bit?"

She nodded.

He opened his mouth to say something more and she headed him off, knowing he was about to broach to subject of last night.

"Don't," she warned. "Let's just leave it as it is. Okay?"

"Okay." He pressed a kiss to her forehead. She swallowed hard pulled out of his arms. "See you later?"

"You will."

At the hospital, he found Malcolm's bed empty when he got to his room, his few things they'd brought over for him packed neatly in a bag on his bed.

Ben felt a moment of panic at the sight of the empty bed. But as he turned back to the nurse's station, he saw Malcolm in his street clothes, walking slowly down the hall with the help of a cane and a nurse—that same one he'd seen him with before. Kelly something. They were laughing at something he said, heads together.

Could he be getting released so soon?

At the nurses' station, he inquired.

"He is, Doctor." The charge nurse, a middle-aged, no-nonsense woman named Helen set aside the chart she was working on. "He's healed up incredibly quickly. He's already a few days ahead of what his doctor had expected and so, he discharged him ten minutes ago. Kelly attributes it to that 'magic' feather his daughter gave him. But between you and me, I think he's a little sweet on her. You know, love heals all things."

Find someone to love.

Malcolm caught sight of Ben and waved, limping toward him. Mal looked better than he had in a year or more… since Patsy. Maybe what he'd needed most was her permission to go and find someone new.

"Ben! Hey! Look at this. They're springing me today! I was just going to call you."

"That's great," he said, meaning it. But what that meant for him and Eve loomed darkly in his mind. "I'm happy for you. That was some fast healing."

"I got excellent care here," he said, smiling at Kelly, who blushed in return. "I feel really good. And I guess my head is harder than they thought. No damage done there."

"Are you here to take him home?" Kelly asked.

"Well, I… have you all sorted out with the stuff at home? Lily? The stock?"

"I've been on the phone the last two days lining up the help I need. I've hired a nanny full time to help me with Lily for the next month or so, and a wrangler I know to tend the stock until I finish up rehab. You're off the hook, officially, man. I can't tell you how much I appreciate all your help. And Eve, too. Is she here?" He glanced behind Ben to look for her and Lily.

"No, she's got Lily making snow angels back at your place. But you can tell her thanks yourself when I take you home. She's enjoyed Lily a lot and will be sad to see that time with her come to an end. Me, too, to be honest."

Malcolm smiled, fingering the feather around his neck. "But I'm sure you must be anxious to get back to work."

"Yeah," he said, but for the first time in a long, long time, that wasn't exactly the truth.

"Word on the floor is you're heading off to the jungles of Honduras," he said. "Is that right?"

"Looks that way. Yeah. I am. But, listen. We did have one more thing to do with Lily. The caroling. We already promised her… so…"

"Sure. Absolutely. She's crazy about you two. And I couldn't appreciate you more. But I don't want to put you out any more than I already have. I can call a cab to take me home."

"No way. I planned on heading back there anyway after tying up a thing or two. I'll take you back. Your paperwork all ready to go?"

"Yup."

"Then," he said to Kelly, "if you're ready to kick him out of here, you two can meet me downstairs at the entrance. And use a wheelchair."

TEN MINUTES LATER, they were headed back to the ranch. Malcolm stretched his leg out in the front seat of Ben's Lexus.

"I never imagined a knock on the head and a couple of broken bones would be exactly what I needed to pull me out of that dark place I've been in since Patsy, but they were. Maybe that and her Christmas list, reminding me that life has to go on. She knew it, even at the end of hers."

"Patsy was a special woman."

"And I'll never stop loving her. But she said it. Find someone to love. And I realized I'd been putting all my love into Lily and that's too much responsibility for any one child to carry. And I liked being married. I miss it. I miss the friendship we had."

This was not a conversation Ben wanted to have right now. Not when he had just chosen the exact opposite track for his own life. Aloneness rather than the possibility of love. So he changed the subject and told Malcolm about the new foal. His eyes lit up and he thanked Ben profusely.

"I don't honestly know how I would have gotten through this whole thing without you and Eve. I am very lucky to have friends like you."

"As it turned out, it was a good break for both of us. I was glad to be there to help with the foal. She's a little beauty, too." As he spoke the words, his thoughts turned to Eve and what had happened between them last night. Just the memory tightened a curl of desire in him again. She'd been on his mind all morning and now, he feared, she'd stay there for good.

No one gets out unscathed.

The frigid Montana landscape glittered under the afternoon sun as they headed down the highway. In the distance, the Absarokas loomed, a hazy grey-blue, fingering up toward the sky. He guessed he would miss that when he left.

"I'm gonna ask that nurse, Kelly, out when I'm well," Malcolm told him. "I liked her."

"If I don't miss my guess, the feeling was more than mutual," he said. "Why wait?"

He straightened. "You're right. Maybe I won't wait. But, just so you know, she was strictly professional," he said quickly. "Don't misunderstand."

"It's none of my business, Mal," he assured him. "I'm outta there. And I'm the last person who should be judging anyone about their relationships."

Mal stared out the window, watching the landscape slide by. "I just didn't want you to think she did anything wrong. She was kind to me when I needed some kindness. But maybe there's more to it than that. I hope so." He cracked open the window, glad to be out of the hospital and breathing fresh air, no doubt.

"I hope so, too," Ben said, but he wasn't thinking about Kelly.

EVE AND LILY were laughing, having used up most of the

fresh powder from last night's gentle snowfall in the yard making snow angels and they had moved on to building a snowwoman. They'd built her the same height as Lily and gathered up some of her outgrown things to decorate her—a straw hat from summer, a winter scarf, an old pair of mittens perched on her stick arms. When they'd finished decorating her face with baby carrots, beets and Halloween wax candy lips, they walked over to the fence line to feed the rest of the carrots to the horses.

It was a comparatively warm morning for December and icicles, hanging from the wood fence, dripped with little prisms of sunshine.

"I wish Mommy could see our snow girl," Lily said, holding a carrot on her flat palm to one of the horses. "She liked snow girls."

"I bet she did," Eve replied. "I bet she's watching right now, giving you a high five."

"Really?" A little grin lifted her small mouth.

"I bet."

"Sometimes," Lily said, "she talks to me at night, when I'm sleeping."

Eve blinked and looked away.

"Sometimes she even lets me hug her."

Eve tucked an arm around the child and pulled her close. "That's so nice," she said. "You're lucky you get to visit with her now and then."

"I know." Her voice was small. "Do you think she'll ever

come home someday?"

Oh, dear. "I think… she's always here, around you, Lily. She always will be. And if you talk to her, she'll hear you. Just look at the feather she gave you, because she needed you to know she was there."

Solemnly, Lily patted the nose of the gelding blowing a steamy breath near her hand. "My friend, Ellie in preschool says there's no such thing as angels. Except on top of Christmas trees."

Eve bumped her shoulder gently with her own. "But, hey, we know better, don't we?"

Lily nodded, feeding her last carrot to the mare pushing her way past the others. "And even though I don't have my feather, she's still here, right?"

"Definitely. No matter what."

Lily turned at the sound of a car pulling into the driveway. "Daddy!" With all the grace of a four-year-old, arms and legs flailing, she raced toward Ben's car where Malcolm occupied the passenger seat.

Eve smiled and waved at them and slowly began walking toward the car. It was with mixed emotions she watched Malcolm return home, knowing this time together—their little pretend family—was coming to an end. Despite last night, she wasn't ready yet. She hadn't prepared. Yet she couldn't help but feel happy for Lily that her father was back where he belonged and that he looked… happy. The little girl needed him now more than ever.

Christmas was, indeed, a time of miracles and if ever anyone needed proof, Malcolm's quick recovery was it.

Her gaze flicked to Ben. He met her look with a stark one of his own. This was the beginning of their end. Better to rip the bandage off quickly than try to spare themselves the long, slow sting.

She'd known this… thing between them was only temporary, just like his feelings for her probably were. Soon, he would move on, back to the life he'd known. Medicine, medicine, and more medicine. And the jungles of Honduras.

To keep from blubbering like an idiot, she forced a smile and walked Malcolm into the house where he marveled at the decorations and the tree, and Lily showed him all of her hard work, especially what was left of the Christmas cookies. When she was out of earshot, Eve promised Mal she'd go shopping for Christmas gifts for her and help him wrap them.

Ben disappeared upstairs to pack. Apparently, he couldn't get out fast enough.

And though she'd sworn she wouldn't let it happen, Eve felt her heart break a little bit.

MALCOLM RELUCTANTLY STAYED home while they took Lily caroling with a handful of friends gathered at the last minute. Finn and Kate came with their kids, and their friends from school, the Baxters, a young professional couple with three kids under the age of eight.

They strolled down Main Street beneath the street lights and stopped where shoppers were stocking up for the holidays. They sang the simple carols with the children—"Jingle Bells", "Silent Night", "Away in a Manger". Some that the children didn't know, the adults sang, following along on the printed out lyrics Kate had made for them. Shopkeepers and customers alike welcomed them, charmed by the children, all red-cheeked and trundled up in their scarves, hats, and winter coats. Everyone stopped to listen and applauded them when they'd finished.

For his part, Ben hummed along except for the most familiar of carols and made sure they had all the kids as they made their way from store to store. That, and taking a video for Malcolm so he could share in the fun. Lily was in her element and he couldn't help but remember the frightened child he'd seen that first night in the hospital and compare her to this ebullient one.

Eve was a natural with her, whispering the lyrics to her when she didn't know them, Lily's small hand in hers at all times. Someday, she would be a great mother.

Not for the first time, Ben found himself pondering that image and trying to fit himself into that picture, beside her. Him, a father, whose own father had been nothing more than a shadow of a parent. To say he'd never imagined what he'd be like as a father would be a lie. But his vision for his life had always been medicine and medicine alone. This week, had been the first in a long time when he wasn't day-in, day-out obsessed with his work. But the balance of a real life with that… he wasn't at all sure how to make such a thing work.

Eve laughed at something her brother-in-law, Finn, said as they walked toward their next destination.

He'd half expected her to avoid him tonight and act as if nothing had happened between them. Another woman would have, and probably wisely so. But that wasn't the choice she made. Instead she included him, touched him without self-consciousness and laughed like there was no tomorrow. He should have known better. Eve Canaday filled up every moment with life.

They all stopped for hot chocolate at Sage's again when they were done. Sage topped the hot drinks with marshmallows and the kids got busy counting, just to be sure they hadn't been shortchanged.

"You're coming for Christmas Eve at Lane's End, Ben, aren't you?" Kate asked as they warmed their hands on their drinks. "Please say you will. You must."

He'd told Eve he would. "I'll make my best effort," he said, though he usually worked Christmas Eve to give other doctors time with their families. "I'll definitely try."

Eve smiled a little sadly before turning her attention to the children, fussing with Lily's scarf.

"I'll hold you to that," Finn said.

"We always have at least thirty people there, sometimes

more and it's great fun," Kate said. "We'll make sure Malcolm and Lily come this year, too."

"And if he gets really lucky," Eve added, "Maybe Kelly will come as well."

Maybe this year, he'd make an exception to working on Christmas. Maybe just this once, he'd pretend they were his family and he deserved a holiday with them, too.

Later, they stood in Eve's driveway, saying goodnight. He'd driven her back from Malcolm's and now was the moment he'd been dreading for days.

"Thank you," he said, "for helping me with Lily. For everything. I really enjoyed these past few days." He shook his head. "That kind of sounds all wrong when I say it out loud."

"You're welcome," she said, unable to look him in the eye.

He rubbed his hands up and down her arms, wanting to pull her toward him, but waiting for some sign she wanted that.

Snow began falling lightly again, pattering against their faces with little whispers. Light from the streetlamps slanted against the snow on her walkway.

"I wish…" he began, but faltered into silence.

"You wish?" She looked up through her lashes now.

"Never mind."

"Tell me."

"I wish I could be the man you needed."

She sighed and looked off into the darkness. "Never mind. I know you've decided."

She would find someone. Some other man who would be what she needed. But even as that thought coalesced, a sharp tug of jealousy ripped through him that it wouldn't be him. But why not him? Why had he taken that damned job now?

But his taking the job was only a symptom of his fear of commitment. To anything outside of medicine. Or maybe it was his fear of tangling someone else up in his messed up history.

She bowed her head. "It's probably best, Ben, if we just… let it go."

A muscle jumped in his jaw and he squinted, looking away. "I'm not leaving just yet. Maybe—"

"Really," she said. "We're grown-ups, Ben. Shit happens. And people say goodbye."

He grabbed her hand as she started to turn away and pulled her palm to his lips. Pressing a lingering kiss there, with his eyes slammed shut. "I'm sorry."

"I know." She swallowed thickly and looked away. "And I don't mean to un-invite you to the Christmas Eve bash. Of course, you should come. And we'll all celebrate. As friends. Which is, after all, what we are."

But he wasn't sure that was true anymore, either.

Chapter Twelve

THE NEXT FEW days dragged by for Eve. Ben had called twice, but she hadn't returned his calls. She just couldn't. What was left to say? Even though he'd asked her to go to Honduras with him, never once had he said the words that might have enticed her to go. Not that she wanted to go there. And she wasn't, frankly, even sure he did. But he didn't love her. Despite her best efforts. So that was that.

Though she tried to stay busy with work, planning the few events upcoming in the next month, her heart wasn't in it. Neither was her head. So she spent her time shopping for Lily with a list Malcolm provided and she and Malcolm wrapped gifts after Lily went to bed.

The nanny he'd hired was working out well, though Eve couldn't help wishing it was her doing the job, rather than the nanny. She missed tucking Lily in at night and having a little helper to make cookies and meals with. In truth, missing Lily only highlighted the fact that she was alone again, but alone in a way she hadn't really been before.

Lonely.

When Kelly accepted Malcolm's invitation to spend Christmas Eve at the Lane's End bash, she was happy for them both, but perversely miserable for herself. Though she'd reiterated her Christmas Eve invitation to Ben, she felt sure that last kiss, pressed against her palm meant goodbye. And it was a punctuation mark on their time together, if ever there was one. But she'd done it. She'd said goodbye.

Back in her place, out of boredom mostly, Eve pulled out the photos that woman, Ali, had left her the other night, thinking she'd toss them to get rid of clutter. But the photos were good. Better than good. They were… art. She'd done wedding photography, clearly, and done it well. Eve glanced at the resume, which was short and to the point. She listed a former address as Calgary, Canada, but it seemed she was American. The resume included a phone number, but no email.

Eve fanned herself with the resume, pacing the living room. She wouldn't hire this girl. She definitely shouldn't. So why was she even contemplating it? There was, weirdly, something about her…

She shoved the resume back in its envelope and tucked it into a drawer. She'd think about it after the holiday. There was still time to find a photographer in town somewhere, wasn't there?

On the eve of Christmas Eve, she went to a house party thrown by a bunch of old friends, girlfriends, mostly, but a mixed group of couples and singles came. She'd gone to dozens of parties like this in the past and hardly blinked at attending alone. But tonight, for the first time really in a long time, she felt like an odd duck. Everyone seemed coupled up, or if they weren't, they made it a point to hook up there. Or maybe she was just imagining it.

Or missing Ben.

She left early, making her excuses to the hostess and driving out to Lane's End without really pondering her destination. Home felt like something she needed right now and as she walked through the door, the scent of Christmas seeped past the angst of the previous week. The cinnamony-anise potpourri boil Jaycee loved wafted on the air along with the sharp tang of the noble firs that decorated the entry near the front door and in the living room. Even though all of the girls had left home now, Christmas decorations were still a must in this household.

"Evie!" her father exclaimed, lowering the book he was reading before the fire. "What a surprise! Wow, you look beautiful. Where've you been?"

"A party. I left. I didn't really feel like doing that tonight."

"We were invited to one tonight, too, but decided to stay in. We've been to something almost every night this week and we needed to stock the reserves for tomorrow night. So what brings you out here?"

She dropped her coat onto the sofa and flung herself

dramatically across it. "Nothing, really. I just missed seeing you."

"Evie…"

"Okay, I needed to apologize for running out on you at the ball. That was awful of me. I'm sorry."

"Kate got your text and we knew not to worry. Do you want to talk about it?"

"No. I don't. I can't really." She would only end up crying and upsetting them, too. And what was the point in everyone losing it so close to Christmas. "I was wondering if… would you mind too much if I slept over here tonight? I just kind of feel like not being alone. And I can help mom tomorrow with the Christmas Eve party prep."

He put his book aside and straightened, casting a worried look her way. "You don't need an excuse to stay here, darlin'. This is still your home, too. Of course you can stay. And she'd love your help. Why don't you go say 'hi?' She's in the kitchen making pumpkin bread."

Her stepmom looked up as Eve wandered into the kitchen. "Hey, you! What a lovely surprise."

"Oh, yeah. That's me. I'm just full of surprises these days."

"You alone?" she asked, looking past her, presumably for Ben.

"Not anymore," she said with a wink, dipping her finger in the cream cheese frosting for a lick. "Oh, God, that is good."

"Hey! Fingers out!"

Sugar always distracted her from whatever life could throw at her. "I am here to serve. Dad said I could spend the night. You don't mind, do you? I wouldn't want to interfere with anything… you know…"

"Nope. Not at all." She winked. "And I need a party slave. You are here in that capacity, right?" she teased.

"Absolutely."

"I mean when your own daughter is the best party designer in town—" Jaycee looked up at Eve who was fighting back sudden, irrational tears. "Honey, what is it? Is it Ben?"

Eve slumped onto a bar stool at the counter. "Gosh, can't a girl just get hormonal without everyone assuming it's all about a boy? It's just this holiday. I'm beginning to understand why people dread it."

Jaycee stirred the frosting thoughtfully. "Christmastime is fraught, that's for sure," she admitted, taking care not to step on Eve's privacy. "Come on. Help me frost the pumpkin bread. My no fail cure for the holiday blues. Olivia's coming in the morning to help, too. If we finish early, maybe we can all take the horses up to the ridge and back. Just to get out."

"I'd love that, Mom. I really would." She wasn't sure if "getting out" would cure what ailed her, or clear Ben Tyler from her cobwebby mind, but the fresh air of a ride always set her head straight when she felt discombobulated. The alternative—dwelling on love, unrequited—felt substantially less appealing. Time to kick that old can down the road.

BEN'S PHONE RANG at dark-thirty a.m. and he reached automatically for it, assuming it was the hospital with some emergency. Instead, the voice on the other end of the line sounded distant and vaguely familiar.

"Dr. Tyler? You awake? Angus, here."

That Dr. Camran was calling him this early in the morning had Ben bolting straight up in bed. He ran a hand down his face. Fatigue jumbled his thoughts. Wasn't the man in the depths of the jungles by now? What was he doing calling him on the morning of Christmas Eve?

"Yes. Yes, I'm awake. Hello, Angus."

"So verra sorry to bother you at this hour, but it seems we have a situation down here that bears a conversation. I know you hadn't planned on coming permanently until after the first of the year, but we had to return to base unexpectedly as one of our doctors has taken ill with something quite rare. As we speak, we've hired a private jet to fly him up to Seattle to a specialist there and that leaves us short, as you can imagine. We were talking, the team and myself, and we wondered if we sent that private jet your way from Seattle, later today, if you'd consider coming down a bit early. It would save you all the bother of commercial flights and get you down here in comfort. Most importantly, quickly."

He shoved a hand through his sleep-spiked hair. "You…

you want me to leave here tonight?"

"I know it's terribly short notice," Camran said, "but if you can make it to the Bozeman airport by five, we'll have the jet waiting for you. I'm afraid this will be your only chance to come down this way and you were planning on coming in ten days or so..."

Ben's mind spun with the possibilities, colliding with his waffling decision to go or not to go to Eve's parents' Christmas party tonight. He'd been leaning heavily to "no" as she'd made it clear she wanted to move on, which was, undoubtedly, the best choice for her. And he'd spent the last few days wrapping up loose ends at the hospital, not taking on new patients. But leaving at all had become a question in his mind as the days stretched by without seeing Eve. Irrational as it was, he'd contemplated changing his mind. But he'd missed that boat, apparently and she was finished with him. His calls to her had gone unanswered.

"I didn't really expect..." he began, fumbling for a reason to say no. "I'm not exactly—"

Camran shot back a list of reasons why this made sense for him. But even as he spoke, Ben tuned him out, knowing he'd made his decision more than a week ago to go there. It was all a matter of time. He'd miss the Christmas party, but that would probably suit Eve anyway. He didn't want to spoil Christmas for her.

Shit.

"All right," he said, before he could change his mind.

"I'll do it. I'll be at the airport by five p.m."

"Brilliant! You sure now?"

Was he? Hell no. He wasn't sure about anything in his life anymore. "I'll start packing right away."

"We'll have the jet waiting for you at hanger 2B." He went on, giving Ben details about where to meet them at the airport in Honduras, but Ben wasn't really listening. He was trying to imagine how he'd say goodbye to Eve.

LATER THAT AFTERNOON, Ben pulled his car into the curving driveway at Lane's End, having tracked Eve down here through Jake and Olivia when he found her not at her own home. On a perfect Montana Christmas Eve, the sun was shining crisp and bright, the trees were dusted with snow and from inside the house Christmas music played. He stood on the porch for a long moment before knocking, contemplating his words. He couldn't leave without saying goodbye, but she wasn't answering her phone. Either she'd left it behind or she was deliberately ignoring his calls.

Probably the latter.

Before he could raise his fist to knock on the door, it opened.

"Ben," Reed said, surprised to see him. "You're early. The party's not for a few hours."

"I'm looking for Eve, actually. Is she here? I left a few messages, but haven't been able to reach her."

"She is." Reed rubbed his jaw. "But with winter still being so mild, the girls all took a ride up to the ridge on horseback since the snow's not too deep yet. Left about an hour ago. I'm holding down the fort and timing the food. Want to come in and wait for her?"

Damn. He glanced up toward the ridge but couldn't spot them. His luck. "I can't stay, actually. I'm on my way out of town and I've got to catch a plane."

The older man frowned. "Really? Not Honduras already?"

"The schedule got bumped. One of the other doctors took ill."

"So… you're going to miss the party." Not a question. An unhappy statement.

"Unfortunately, yes. But I wanted to tell Eve goodbye."

"I guess it won't come as a big surprise to her. But I'll tell her you stopped by. She'll be sorry she missed you."

He wasn't so sure that was true, but nonetheless, it felt wrong to leave without seeing her. This morning's phone call had rushed him into a timeframe that left no room for error.

"Tell her…" Ben began, shoving his hands into the pockets of his shearling coat. "Tell her I'm sorry we couldn't say goodbye in person. Tell her I'll call her."

Reed stuck his hand out to Ben and he took it. "I will."

He turned to go, but Reed's words stopped him.

"Piece of advice, Ben? I know you didn't ask for it, but here it is. Ambition is a good thing. I'm ambitious. Always have been. It's gotten me far in what I do. But in the end, ambition is a cold lover who will never care about you the way you do her. And she will leave you wishing you'd seen her for what she really was, instead of the thing that makes you whole." He shoved his hands into the pockets of his jeans, his breath, white with the cold. "Good luck with the new job. We'll miss you around here."

Taken aback by Reed's unsolicited counsel, he slid his look away from the older man's scrutiny and almost laughed to think of what his own father—the advocate of unfettered ambition—would think of such advice? He could just imagine. He supposed it was a fair assumption that ambition was what was driving him to Honduras, too. Though he could no longer delude himself that it was the only thing.

Above the yard, with a flash of red, a cardinal circled a birdfeeder already swarming with sparrows.

"Merry Christmas, Mr. Canaday."

Reed smiled down at him. "And to you, son."

TWILIGHT CAME EARLY in December, and from the backseat of the town car he'd hired to take him to the airport, Ben watched the Christmas glow of Marietta disappear behind them.

On the way out of town, he'd seen families heading in to church or to house parties, carrying casseroles and gifts. Everyone in their place and a place for everyone.

Stop feeling sorry for yourself, Tyler. You had your chance and you blew it. Without you, their world will keep spinning just fine and you'll be in another hemisphere. Keep your eyes on the path. Don't look up.

But he couldn't help but think of Eve's party, already underway, and he watched the road spin by, imagining her there. That sexy, little lift at the corner of her mouth she had whenever she saw him—the one he'd misread for so many months—that said *I see you*. The sparkle in her eyes and the mischief that spelled. He imagined her walking up to him and kissing him in the midst of that crowd, not caring what any of them thought. He could almost taste her.

Despite the ache that fantasy ignited in his groin, his gut clenched as well.

She'd taken over his thoughts over these past few weeks like some kind of avalanche, picking up speed as time passed, tumbling him around inside of her ideas about who and what he could be.

Reed's admonition about ambition lingered in his mind, too. God knew, he'd operated on ambition since he could remember, but he knew only too well that medicine would not keep him warm at night or comfort him, if he ever admitted to needing such a thing. Medicine had become his shelter, his refuge. But it would not always be so. And the ambition that had driven Ben to look further than his own backyard felt suddenly unappealing. But that was the path he'd taken.

"You okay back there?" his driver asked, glancing at him

in the rear view mirror. "I have some water if you'd like some."

"I'm fine, thanks."

"Looks like a nice clear shot for Christmas Eve to the airport."

He glanced up at the driver whose name was Bruce, a middle-aged man, of medium build, with a friendly face, he looked like he must have a family somewhere. "Did I take you away from your holiday, driving me tonight?"

"No worries, Doc. My wife and kids are used to me driving all hours. We'll celebrate later, when I get home. We usually go to a midnight mass up in Livingston. Anyway, I'm grateful for the job. Must be tough for you though, having to take off on a Christmas Eve."

"I suppose," Ben answered. A few weeks ago, nothing could have been further from the truth. But now… Watching the highway speed by in the gloaming dark, his thoughts landed on Patsy's last letter.

Find someone to love.

His cell phone rang and he reached for it, his heart raced, thinking it might be Eve. But the caller ID was a number from San Francisco. And he guessed who it was.

"Benjamin?" said a familiar deep voice on the other end.

"Hello, Father," he said, disappointed. "This is a surprise."

"Is it? Well, it's Christmastime. And a colleague happened to mention to me that you'd accepted a post somewhere down in Central America. Is that true?"

"It is." But he wondered how the word had gotten out so quickly and who'd told him.

Outside his window, the starry Montana sky twinkled over the snow-covered pass as they climbed.

"Well, good for you, getting out of Marietta," his old man was saying. "I warned you about going back, didn't I? I see I was right. You can never go back home."

"Right about what, Father? Remind me."

The elder Dr. Tyler chuckled. "I don't suppose I have to since you're leaving, but you know you'll never achieve what you want there. Small town, small minds, small budgets. It's a terminal position. And it will never go anywhere for you."

"Actually," he said, staring out the window, "I found it just the opposite. Good people who want to help, who care about you, whether you deserve it or not."

A low growling sound came from the other end. "Don't get caught up in all that, Benjamin. This operation in Honduras, I've looked them up. Dr. Camran has quite a reputation and is well published in all the journals. I foresee a published article or two coming out of this experience for you as well. And it won't look bad on your curriculum vitae, either. Altruism always benefits a well-rounded C.V."

"What are you doing for Christmas this year?" Ben asked, wanting to change the subject.

"Taking a little time on a beach in Maui with Jemma. We're heading there now."

Right. He'd heard of Jemma. Half his father's age and not interested in marriage.

"I think your mother is in London," the old man was saying. "Though she doesn't confide all the pertinent details of her life back there with me."

Ben was only half-listening, remembering the warmth of the Canady kitchen, the smell of holiday cooking. Reed's advice.

"Benjamin? Are you still there? Is anything wrong, son?"

It was a question so out of the ordinary, Ben blinked and met the driver's eyes in the rear view mirror. "No. I'm fine." *I've just royally screwed up my life is all.* "Why do you ask?"

"You don't sound yourself." Another pause. "You didn't get yourself involved with a woman, did you? Not at this stage of your career?"

"Involved?" Ben stared out the window at the drifts of snow in the fields off the highway twinkling with starlight. "Yes. Yes, I did get involved with a woman. A really good woman. And I hurt her."

"Oh… well," his father blustered, "not to worry. For the best. A sea full of fish and all that and a career to build." Then he muttered something reassuring and muffled to Jemma who was apparently filling the space beside his old man. "You certainly don't want to be chained to a place like Marietta for years like I was."

"I gotta go, Father. Have a nice holiday at the beach."

"Oh. All right. Good luck in Honduras. Keep in touch.

Merry Christmas, son."

"To you, too." And he hung up.

He stared down at his phone, scrolling through his photographs. Pictures of Lily feeding reindeer, Eve on the sleigh ride. The lights on Malcolm's house as Eve and Lily danced inside. All moments he would only have pictures to remind him of. He tightened the focus on a photo of Eve and a muscle clenched in his jaw.

Outside, the dark road rimmed the mountain pass, opening here and there to the view below. The moon was nearly full and moonlight bounced off a shiny surface below in the distance.

"Stop the car," he told Bruce. "Pull over here, would you?"

"What? Are you sick?"

Maybe. "No. Just… please. Stop the car."

He did and Ben got out. Outside, the air slapped him cold and crisp. He buttoned his coat up, scanning the near darkness of the field just off the road. He climbed up the low bank of snow at the edge of the meadow and the foothills parted to reveal Miracle Lake in the distance, the rising moon spilling across the icy surface like a headlamp.

He sucked in a breath at the sight. There was, indeed, something miraculous about it, and he thought he'd never seen anyplace so beautiful before. He remembered the story Lane Carson had told about the lake and the powers it held. Standing here, one could almost believe that about a place as beautiful as that one.

Almost instinctively, he wanted to turn to Eve and share the view with her. But of course, he couldn't. But neither could he move one foot further toward Honduras when leaving felt so irrevocably wrong.

"*The things you do have consequences, Ben, no matter what your intention.*"

Leaving her was… intentional. An act of pure cowardice. And the consequences of that act would reverberate through his life for years to come. Years without her. Whatever he achieved, whatever good things happened to him, he couldn't imagine them feeling anything but hollow without her to share them with.

He didn't want to go. Or go without her.

No. Scratch that. Whatever reasons he'd had for going in the first place had been exploded by a girl who loved Christmas, who brightened a room just by walking into it. And he could not believe it had taken him so long to understand how she'd changed him.

But what if she's really finished with you? What if you're too late? What if your leaving tonight was her last straw?

Are you too much of a coward to find out? Will you just stand on the other side of that moat and always wonder?

Eve made him want to be more than what he'd become on his own. He'd even begun to imagine having children with her. A little girl like Lily who would take his hand in hers and trust him. A child who would never feel alone or wonder if she was loved. He'd always thought that part of him was broken, but even he could see now that broken things could be mended. Moats could be crossed. Trying didn't come without risk, but what did that was worth anything?

He needed to go back, dammit, and face the consequences. And hope she'd give him one last shot.

From somewhere overhead, he heard the heavy swoop of wings. He looked up, and saw nothing but a pure, white feather drifting down from above him, landing nearly on his nose. He reached and caught it between his hands, staring down at it in disbelief.

No.

Couldn't be.

Could it?

Find someone to love.

Maybe that note had been meant for him and Malcolm both. In fact, he was sure it was.

He brushed the vanes of the feather with his fingertips and smiled up at the stars.

"Thanks, Patsy," he whispered, emotion choking his throat. "You always did have a good eye."

He heard the driver get out of the car behind him and he turned back, walking down the hill through the snow.

"You okay up there?" the man called.

Ben joined him on the road. "I am."

"Hey, Doc, you won't believe this, but a reindeer just

crossed the road right in front of my car. A real reindeer! On Christmas Eve! Wait 'til I tell my kids. A minute either way and we might've hit it. It just stood there, you know, looking at me with those big eyes in the middle of the road for a minute before it just… walked off."

But the animal was gone now. Vanished. As usual.

"You weren't meant to hit it, Bruce," he said, still staring down at the feather. "You were meant to see it."

"Beg pardon?"

"It was the universe talking. Or… an old friend of mine." He turned to look at the man. "Anyway, it's Christmas Eve and I'm supposed to be somewhere else."

The driver looked at him sideways. "Well, then. Okay. We best get back on the road. Don't want you to miss your flight."

"Bruce?" Ben walked back toward the car and shook the man's hand. "Merry Christmas. How'd you like to get back home in time for the nine o'clock Mass in Livingston?"

EVE REFILLED A nearly empty tray of cheesecake tartlets for the dessert table, hardly feeling in the spirit at all. Beyond the kitchen door, she heard the sounds of the crowd of guests laughing and talking, already choosing gifts from the greedy bingo table and arguing steals and trades. She'd drawn the number thirty-five and they weren't nearly at that number yet. So she lingered in the kitchen, listening to the piped in

Christmas music.

"He stopped by to say goodbye," her father had told her when they'd come back from the ridge. "Said he tried to call you, but you didn't answer."

Because she'd deliberately been ignoring her phone today. Heartache had rocketed through her, even though she'd half expected as much. Just as well. She swallowed her disappointment that he wasn't going to come tonight, surprised that he was leaving so soon. She managed not to cry. But she wasn't sure she could have borne saying goodbye to him in person. No need to drag it out. They'd virtually said their goodbyes a few days ago, after Lily's. It was over and that was that.

The kitchen smelled so good. She inhaled the scent of Christmas and decided to pull herself together. What was done was done. The least she could do was enjoy her parents' party. She popped a cheesecake tartlet in her mouth. Whole.

"Evie, come out. You're missing greedy bingo." Olivia said, bursting through the kitchen door, grabbing the tray from her. "Oooh, busted with the cheesecake tarts!"

Eve managed to swallow the mouthful, covering her mouth with her hand. "I just had one. But… maybe I'll have another," she announced, grabbing one off the tray. "Or two. Maybe even three."

"Whoa, Nelly! Step away from the sugar carbs. No man is worth that."

Ben might just be.

But she sighed and said, "You're right. You're absolutely right." She put the tartlets back and pushed Olivia back toward the door. "Here. Take them out of here. I don't want to look at them. Wait. Just one more." She snatched one, popped it in her mouth and sent Olivia a guilty grin. "Go."

Her sister shook her head. "C'mon. Come join us. You're gonna miss your number being called. It's Christmas."

She pulled the small, handwritten number on the small piece of paper out of her pocket. "Here. You pick something for me. Or steal something. I'm really not in the mood. I just need a minute."

Olivia sent her a sympathetic look. "Okay. But if you're not out there in five, I'm coming back here to get you."

Eve wiped down the counters and straightened the kitchen, knowing this kind of busywork was just the thing to take her mind off him. Not that it actually worked, but at least she wasn't sitting still, feeling sorry for herself.

Her thoughts rewound, as they'd been doing for the better part of this week, around each and every detail of their time together, wondering what she might have done differently to change the outcome. Not the least of which was what had happened with him the night of the ball. After the ball. But there was no rationale that would have changed their course. In hindsight, she wouldn't change it. Yes, he'd wounded her by going, regardless of what they'd shared, but she'd known that going in. She was no victim and he was no villain. Nor was his leaving her fault. She had done nothing wrong. He'd simply made a choice.

She would survive. It wouldn't kill her. She was stronger than that. But allowing herself a few tears was the least she could do.

Wiping a hand over her cheek, she straightened her dress, took off the apron and pushed through the swinging door to the living room.

"Number thirty-five!" her father, the emcee of the greedy bingo game was calling. "Anyone have it?" The guests craned their necks to see who was next to draw a wrapped gift from the crowded table.

That was her number. But she'd given it to Olivia, who was watching her with a strange expression. Eve lifted her hands as if to say, *what the heck? Go*!

"I've got number thirty-five," a deep voice said from across the room.

Pulling her gaze past the familiar guests who were drinking hot cider and laughing, she saw him.

"Ben!" Reed said, surprised, trading looks with Jaycee and Eve. "Come on in. You can choose from the table or steal from one of the gifts already opened. Your choice."

He met her gaze over the heads of the guests and Eve felt heat climb up her cheeks. She wasn't sure how to react. Her knees, though, they were quite confidently shaking.

"Merry Christmas, Reed. Everyone." Ben eased through the crowd toward the table. "I don't want to pick from there and there's nothing that I want to steal. So"—he wound around the gift table, closer to where she was standing—"I pick Eve. She's my pick. If she's willing, that is."

Eve's mouth dropped open and she exchanged shocked looks with her father and sisters. Almost everyone else seemed delighted by this turn of events and some even clapped at his choice. Reed watched Ben with a little frown of wariness.

She swallowed thickly. "I—Ben, I—" All eyes were on them and she couldn't do this in front of a crowd.

It was too complicated for a simple answer. She was no greedy bingo gift and he was supposed to be on his way to Honduras. He opened his mouth to say more, but she stopped him.

"Don't"—she warned, holding up one finger—"say another word. Come with me." She turned on her heel and headed back into the kitchen as murmur rose behind her. Why, dear God, did he have to do this again, in front of everyone?

When he followed her into the kitchen she faced him, arms folded protectively across her chest. "What are you doing here, Ben? I thought you left." Dressed in jeans and a flannel shirt, sleeves rolled up his forearms, he loomed over her, standing not three feet away. She leaned backward, against the sink, using it for support.

"I started to go," he admitted, "but I changed my mind."

Keeping her expression carefully blank, she said, "Delayed your trip, did you?"

"Indefinitely. Permanently." He slid his Sherpa coat over the back of a kitchen chair and moved closer.

"I… I thought you were bound to go."

"I'm not actually bound to do anything but what I want to do. And what I want to do is to stay here with you." He pulled a white feather that looked suspiciously like Lily's from his pocket and twirled it between his fingers.

She frowned at it. "But what about—Is that Lily's?"

"No. I got one of my very own. Standing in a field overlooking Miracle Lake. Some kind of… cosmic machination, I guess." A grin tipped his mouth. "Or Patsy."

She blinked. "But you don't believe in—"

"There's all kinds of things I didn't used to believe in. A man can change, can't he?"

"Maybe," she answered in a small voice, trying to keep the hope from it. "If he really wants to. For himself. What are you saying, Ben?"

"I'm saying, only a shortsighted man doesn't believe in little bit of magic." He reached for a strand of hair that had fallen in her eyes and tucked it behind her ear. "And only a fool walks away from the best thing that's ever happened to him."

She shook her head and started to turn away.

"I've been doing a lot of thinking," he said, insisting that she listen. "In the last few days since you've been gone. Since we…" He cleared his throat. "Since that last night. I figured

I'd blown it all with you, since you wouldn't return my calls, wouldn't see me. And maybe that's still true. I understood it, really. So I said yes to Dr. Camran's last minute call to come down tonight on that private jet.

"When I didn't find you here, I thought, maybe it was just as well that we didn't see each other before I left, because it would be easier. Less painful all the way around. Because—well, that's what I do. And I really saw that tonight. And suddenly, I realized on the way to the airport, I didn't want less painful. I wanted all of it. The good, the bad, the easy times and the hard, and I wanted to feel all of those things, but I wanted to feel them with you."

Eve bowed her head and bit her lip. Her throat felt swollen.

"'Cause without you, Eve, all the rest—whatever I achieve, whatever I accomplish—feels irrelevant. You were right about me. I'm closed off and scared of more than I want to admit. But I'll be damned if I'm going to live my father's life. If I'll let him stop me from trying to live my own. But I'm telling you right now, I'll mess up, and then I'll try harder. And I'll keep trying until I get it right for you. Because I'm in love with you, Eve Canaday. So, I'm not going to Honduras. Not tonight. Not ever if you don't want me to." He swallowed hard when she didn't answer right away. "But if I'm too late… Am I? If you can't see it with me—"

"You," Eve said, interrupting him, moving toward him

to put a hand flat on his chest, "are the most irritating, stubborn, *what-am-I-going-to-do-with-you* kind of man."

She kissed him, hard, pulling him down toward her until he wrapped his arms around her and held her close. Swirling her tongue against his, she found herself remembering the wish she'd made, for him to love her, and could not believe he actually, finally did. There was so much water under their bridge, though, so many stumbles. Was this what love was like? Finding footing in spite of those stumbles?

Her fingers threaded through his hair and she broke the kiss, pressed her cheek against his, and shook her head. "I never expected perfection, crazy. I'm flawed, too, in case you haven't noticed. And I've missed you so much the last few days. I thought maybe I was going crazy. But, Ben, to keep you from going? From doing that thing you want to do in Honduras? I could never do that to you."

"I don't care about the damn jungle."

"You might. You might resent me for keeping you here. It was never my intention."

"In Marietta?" He turned an ear toward the living room and the sound of laughter and friendship. "Just listen to that. Why would I want to leave that? More importantly, *you*. The jungle will always be there. There will always be patients who need help. If I go someday, it'll be brief and maybe you'll come with me, just to see the world. But there's nothing there I'm chasing, Eve. Not anymore. I found what I'm looking for right here. I didn't even know what I had standing right in front of me, until you made me see." He pulled back from her and tipped her chin up to him. "Can you forgive me for being such a—"

She pressed her index finger against his lips. "Big dope? Mm-hmm."

"Yeah?" Ben's eyes actually teared then and he flicked a nervous thumb against his lip. "I promise you won't be sorry. I'll make you happy."

"And I'll make you happy right back." Her eyes watered, too, and her throat was almost too thick for words.

"I want to marry you."

A slow smile curved her lips. "We'll talk about that later. It's Christmas Eve. There must be some mistletoe somewhere in this house, meant just for us."

"I don't think we should mess with the mistletoe," he murmured, kissing the tip of her nose and tucking the feather into his pocket.

"Ahh. You're probably right," she agreed, grinning back at him.

"Merry Christmas, Eve."

"Merry Christmas, Ben."

And as he bent to kiss her, from somewhere outside, the faint jangle of jingle bells sounded.

The End

If you enjoyed *The Christmas Wish*,
you'll love the next book in the series....

The Canadays of Montana

B The Canaday clan is like so many modern families today: blended, flawed and full of love for each other. The series follows the Canaday sisters—Olivia, Kate and Eve—strong yet vulnerable women who have careers and challenges that most of us face as they search for balance in their lives. As is also so often true, their strengths are also their weaknesses when it comes to finding and recognizing true love when it knocks on their door. And with heroes every bit as human—and heroic—as the heroines of these stories, I hope you'll find a little bit of yourself in every one.

Book 1: *A Cowboy to Remember*

Book 2: *Choose Me, Cowboy*

Book 3: *The Christmas Wish*
Now a Hallmark Original Movie Holiday Hearts

Book 4: *A Cowboy to Keep*

More by Barbara Ankrum

The Band of Brother series

Book 1: *Unsung Hero*

Book 2: *Once a Hero*

Book 3: *Unexpected Hero*

About the Author

Barbara Ankrum has a thing for the West and has written both historical and contemporary romances, all set in that magical place. Twice nominated for RWA's RITA Award, her bestselling books are emotional, sexy rides with a touch of humor. Barbara's married and raised two children in Southern California, which, in her mind, makes her a native Westerner. Visit Barbara on Facebook and Twitter@BarbaraAnkrum

Thank you for reading

The Christmas Wish

If you enjoyed this book, you can find more from all our great authors at TulePublishing.com, or from your favorite online retailer.

Made in the USA
Lexington, KY
19 November 2019